Silently entering the house, Sue scanned the first room looking down the barrel of her gun.

The tension was indescribable, knowing that an armed man might be around any corner.

Fear gripped her until her stomach was in knots and she had to tell herself to breathe. But not too loudly! Not to give herself away.

Just enough to stay alive.

MURDER
on the
ERIE CANAL

by

Elly Stevens

1

The rippling steel-blue water of the newly filled Erie Canal held a secret—a dark and disturbing secret that now rested fourteen feet below the waterline on the manmade hydraulic-cement floor. It moved slowly with the undulating water, but not far from where it originated, after being slipped in over the side of an unlit, trolling motorboat. There was no resistance nor was there splashing or a loud disturbance that could wake the dead. No. The night remained silent; the air thick with the humidity that precedes a storm. And the water accepted the gift with a gentle ripple that fanned out before it, too, disappeared with the prize well concealed.

A pair of shifty eyes darted back and forth from the boat to assure anonymity. The vessel was simply a moving shadow in the darkness of the spring night as it purred its way back to the boat launch at low speed. The murderer's heart was racing and breath gasping, temporarily. The heart would soon resume a normal rhythm. The deed was done. Life would go on as it had before. Except for the fear of being caught. This perpetrator would be looking over the left shoulder then the right and studying everyone's words and expressions, just in case they might suspect...

The culprit attached the boat's winch line and cranked it, pulling the boat onto a trailer. The truck and trailer drove away into the night, as raindrops started to fall in an animated pattern on the canal's surface. Drip. Drop. Drip, drip, drop. Ripples appeared, at first. Then the force of the larger drops displaced the water with more intensity. When the rain began in earnest, the canal became an angry bed for its new occupant. Resting in peace? Hardly.

The ominous, dark rain clouds burst open, accompanied by a crackling flash of lightning and a roaring roll of thunder. It seemed that the storm was centered right above this section of the canal, erasing all signs of human activity.

The next morning, as the sun rose with its glorious beauty and warmth, occasional raindrops fell off wet tree leaves and flowering shrubs. The storm was over. People started about their business. All seemed well. But there was one soul unaccounted for. That soul would be missed. Eventually.

A day later, a Missing Person's report was posted on the whiteboard of the local police department and the Monroe County New York's Sheriff's Office. A teenage girl from the Town of Gates was missing.

When a second girl from the same town went missing a few weeks later, a new case file was created by the Perlo Detective Agency, where Sue Gainer had just been hired.

❧ 2 ❧

A month earlier...

A man who looked incredibly like handsome actor Kit Harington of *Game of Thrones* fame was about to tell Sue Gainer that he loved her. With her eyes closed, Sue breathlessly awaited those "three little words" and a loving kiss—when her cell phone buzzed, waking her from the dream. Groaning, Sue said goodbye to her virtual "hunk" who looked sad at the last second before he vaporized. Reaching over to pick up her phone and read the time, which was 8:10 a.m., she answered the incoming call. It was her mom. A few months before, her father had been diagnosed with colon cancer, and now her mom wanted her to come home to help out. "Home" was Rochester, New York, over 400 miles away from her apartment in an old Victorian house near the Atlantic Ocean.

"Sweety, I'm not sure I can do this alone. Is there any chance...? Could you consider...?" An anxious voice stumbled over the correct words.

"Moving back to Rochester?" her caring daughter offered up.

"Well, yes. I hate asking you to uproot yourself."

"It's a good time, Mom. I've been preparing for a change." Sue heard a sigh of relief on the other end of the phone.

It was decided.

Sue, a blonde twenty-six-year-old, had recently been a supply chain assistant at Beeler Printing in Delaware. She had excelled at her job, knowing all the supply processes—what needed to go where and when and by whom—but recently, a restlessness in her job began to gnaw at her. Sue wanted to do more, recalling her involvement in saving her immediate supervisor from a murderer and seeing the assailant put behind bars. Becoming a police officer was an interesting possibility, but her passion was in investigative work.

That led to taking a Criminal Justice course, obtaining her Delaware gun permit, purchasing a 9mm Glock 19 with a 10-round capacity, and spending many hours in target practice.

But now, all that changed. Her immediate need was to focus on her parents. Her mom, a high school math teacher, and her dad, a computer programmer at the University of Rochester, were both retired now. There was a burden of guilt because her mom was alone to handle all of her dad's doctor appointments, treatments, and medications. They were both "up there" in age and Sue was their only child. That meant she had to move to Rochester and postpone the private investigator plans—at least temporarily.

Sue didn't leave behind any love interest in Delaware, but life was lonely without a special person to share things with. He didn't have to look like Kit Harington, but there were other qualifications that were necessary—kindness, honesty, patience, and, of course, love. Perhaps, in this new chapter of her life, the right person just might be around the next corner. It was a pleasant thought, and it gave her something new and exciting to look forward to.

Two weeks later, all her belongings were packed in the cargo area of a rental truck, as well as the carrier holding Butterscotch, her ginger cat, in the passenger space. Sue headed out, feeling anxious and unsure of the future. She sold her bright blue Toyota Corolla and planned to find new wheels after getting settled at her parents' house. Putting her hair in a ponytail and donning her Rochester Red Wings baseball cap and sunglasses, she was now ready for the long road trip.

Driving the New York State Thruway was a breeze. Seven hours later, Sue pulled into the driveway that was more than familiar—it was *home.* There were two exterior lights on either side of the garage and a lamp on a post along the walkway that brightened the way to the front door of the center-entrance colonial. No smell of the ocean here, but there was a scent of lilacs in the air. It was lovely! She took a deep breath in and then rang the doorbell.

Two people with graying hair answered the door. Her mom looked tired, but her dad looked old. Sue knew it was the right decision to come back home.

"Sue! I'm so happy you're here!" her mom Carol Gainer exclaimed as she hugged her.

Next, her dad Jerry put his arms around her and started to cry. Sue began to cry, too. They hugged for a minute more, then Sue excused herself to bring in her cat. Retrieved from the front passenger seat of the truck, Butterscotch meowed loudly.

"This is our new home, kitty!" Sue informed him. Butterscotch wasn't too sure about it, but he'd get a chance to sniff things out and find a place to hide for a while.

Her mom served Sue a warm slice of apple pie with a tall glass of milk. For the next hour, Sue heard the lengthy tale of her dad's diagnosis and his first in a series of grueling treatments for eight weeks. Sue was concerned, but they had caught the cancer early, which was a great relief. Thank God for routine colonoscopies.

Sue took her overnight bag and climbed the stairs to her old bedroom. Nothing had changed. There was still a Rochester Red Wings pennant on the wall, her old books on a shelf, and a worn teddy bear resting on the pillows of the full-sized bed. Picking the bear up tenderly, it brought back a flood of memories from her childhood when life was so full of promise. Not that it still couldn't be.

The mirror on the small dresser reflected an image of an older woman than the last time Sue gazed into that same mirror—older but still beautiful—as the twenty-six-year-old removed her makeup and thought about this major change in her life. Where would it lead? Who would she become? How would her life goals be accomplished? An older reflection, maybe, but the same person. Now was her chance to be something more. Placing the jar of makeup remover on the dresser, Sue headed to the welcoming bed. It had been a long day.

It was difficult to fall asleep. There was an unexpected spring thunderstorm that passed through and the house shook when the storm was overhead.

When all was quiet again, Butterscotch came out from under the bed and curled up next to her. Sue petted him gently and listened to his purr, which eventually sent her to dreamland.

The next morning, a sunbeam came through the curtains about 6:30 a.m. Sue threw off the covers while Butterscotch protested. Changing into her jogging pants, top, headband, and fitness watch, Sue got ready for the first full day in New York. Mornings in May were quite chilly in Rochester, so a nylon jacket was needed. Butterscotch followed her downstairs and circled around Sue's legs as she opened a can of cat food. Her pet devoured it in no time. Once he settled back down, Sue quietly left the house to go jogging on the nearby Erie Canalway Trail.

The Erie Canal was an engineering marvel for its time in the early 1800s, going through mountainous terrain and dense rock by hand and animal power, as well as the use of gunpowder. The first phase of the construction started on July 4, 1817, in Rome, New York, and continued east to the Hudson River. Many wealthy farmers along this stretch of the canal participated in constructing their own portion of the canal. It wasn't until 1825 that the rest of the canal, westward to Lake Erie, including the stretch around Rochester, New York, where Sue lived, was completed. This allowed European immigrants entering the Port of New York easy access, via the Hudson River and then the canal, to the Finger Lakes and new cities on the Great Lakes, as well as to the resource-rich regions of the Midwest. Farmers then had the cash to purchase consumer goods since shipping wheat, corn, and other crops to lucrative East Coast markets became cheaper and put more money in their pockets. Then, in 1862, the canal was widened and deepened for larger barges and more cargo. Additional canals were built to connect to Lake Champlain, Lake Ontario via the Genesee River, and to the Finger Lakes. Again, in 1918, the canal was enlarged to fit wider and deeper boats.

After the completion of the St. Lawrence Seaway in 1959, shipping traffic sharply declined on the canal, as the new passageway gave access to the Great Lakes directly from the Atlantic Ocean. After that, the Erie Canal was used primarily for recreational purposes and tourism.

Today, Sue saw her breath as she jogged east on the canal path, passing a few others with the same idea. It felt good to be outside, getting necessary oxygen to her brain and other organs, while working her muscles. To Sue, it was a requirement for living.

Sue felt a personal connection to the canal because her mom said that her great-grandfather worked on the canal at one time. The lyrics "Low Bridge! Everybody Down" by Thomas S. Allen popped into her head:

I've got an old mule and her name is Sal.
Fifteen years on the Erie Canal
She's a good old worker and good old pal.
Fifteen years on the Erie Canal.
We've hauled some barges in our day,
filled with lumber, coal and hay.
And ev'ry inch of the way I know, from Albany to Buffalo.
Low bridge, ev'rybody down! Low bridge, we must be getting near a town.

You can always tell your neighbor. You can always tell your pal,
If he's ever navigated the Erie Canal.

The Erie Canalway Trail was not the old, dirt path of bygone days where a mule walking alongside the canal would pull a barge of goods from town to town, but a newly paved lane for runners and bicyclists. The state maintained the area along the trail.

The canal had just been filled for the season; there were no boats going by today. It was very quiet and serene. Almost too quiet. She wished there were more people along the path as she was starting to feel uncomfortable, as if someone were watching her. She looked around but saw no one, nor did she hear any threatening sounds. Recalling the words of TV reality crime show hosts, always follow your instincts. If something doesn't feel right, it probably isn't. After checking her fitness watch for the number of steps, she turned around and headed back to her car. Two additional vehicles were parked in the lot now, with bicycles on racks and riders in their gear. It gave her a sense of comfort that others were nearby.

Later that morning, Sue and her parents went to the treatment center, where the staff discussed her dad's condition. They were assured that everything possible was being done to make him healthy again. When they returned home, her dad took a nap while Carol made coffee for the two of them.

"Mom, are you familiar with all the bills and financial stuff?" Sue inquired as they sipped the strong, hot brew.

"Well, I always pay the bills myself, so that's fine, but your dad handles our investments. I really don't

ELLY STEVENS

have a handle on them," Carol admitted. Carol was a
high school math teacher, so she had the skills and
the understanding of bookkeeping and problem-
solving, but investing was another matter. She always
left that up to Jerry, who was Wall Street smart.

"How about car and house maintenance?" added
Sue.

"We had our car inspections during the winter and
the registrations are up to date. The house is old, so
there are always issues, like leaky faucets and non-
working sump pumps. We had a very wet spring this
year."

"Okay. Well, I'll go around the house and make a
list of any problems I see. Then I'll go over them with
Dad."

She continued, "What about wills and a Health
Care Proxy?"

"Had them updated last year," her mom informed
her. It sounded to Sue like everything had been taken
care of.

Her mom asked, "Are you going to look for a job?"

"Probably, since I quit my job a couple of months
ago."

"There's no rush, Sue. You can stay with us as long
as you want."

Sue nodded in agreement. She didn't anticipate a
move soon, at least until her dad was better.

3

Unpacking the truck took more time than it did to load it but, eventually, everything was either in Sue's bedroom or stored in the basement of her parents' home. Her mom followed her to the rental return a few miles away where Sue dropped off the truck.

Sue was anxious to set up her computers and printer before anything else, but everything in the room had to be rearranged to fit the equipment. It was not the space she was used to, nor did she have the privacy she was used to, but it was a small price to pay while her dad needed her.

The weekend rolled around and Sue started a job search. It wasn't like the days when jobs were posted in the Want Ad section of the newspaper. Since everything was done through websites and apps, it took Sue time to scroll through the various listings to see if she qualified or if the companies offered training.

There weren't any jobs available in supply chain—the nearest one was in Syracuse, and she wasn't willing to commute. She felt a bit discouraged and put everything aside temporarily to rethink what she wanted her future to look like.

* * * * *

Every morning Sue continued to take her morning jog along the canal, sometimes going east and sometimes going west. No longer feeling spooked by the unknown, she put the fear in the back of her mind. Today, a white patrol car with a black-and-yellow stripe pulled into the busy parking lot, driving slowly, as though the officer was checking license plates or looking for someone. Curious, Sue sauntered over to the car.

"Looking for someone?" she asked the officer, who was young and very good looking, as well as muscular.

"We had a report of a suspicious person in the area. Have you seen anyone unusual?"

"Not today. But a couple of days ago, I had a feeling that someone was watching me."

He briefly spoke into his radio, then turned his attention back to Sue. "I'm Officer Williams with the Brighton Police Department. I need to take down your information. Do you have an ID on you?" While the state patrolled the Erie Canal waterways, the local police departments assisted by monitoring the roadways along the canal.

"I do." Sue pulled out a Delaware driver's license from her waistband wallet and handed it to him. He ran it through his computer.

"Miss Gainer, will you be a permanent resident of New York now?"

"Yes," she replied casually.

"Don't forget that you have to go to the DMV to get a New York State license within 30 days."

"Oh, I never thought about it. I just moved here. I'll do it tomorrow."

He recorded her new address and brief statement about her recent jog. "Do you run along the canal every day?"

"Yes," she responded, "so far, that is."

"I recommend that you change your route," he warned her. "Stay alert." He handed the Delaware license back to her. She felt goosebumps, thinking about her first run.

"Thanks. I appreciate it." Sue smiled, and the officer smiled back with sparkling white teeth. All during her run, suspicious people were secondary on her mind; the handsome young officer had intrigued her and preoccupied her thoughts.

Later, back at her desk in the bedroom, Sue did an internet search on police activity along the Rochester area of the canal. Surprisingly, there was very little in recent times—mostly graffiti complaints, stolen cars dumped in the canal, crashes, drownings, suicides, and even dog rescues—and a recent story in the paper about the recovery of a body of a teenage girl in the canal. Now *that* was frightening, and it gave her pause.

It also made her think about seeing Officer Williams again.

"It would be interesting to get to know him and pick his mind," Sue thought.

Concerned that her parents might worry, Sue decided not to mention the conversation with Officer Williams or the article about the dead girl. She continued to accompany her father to his treatments and to help her mother in the kitchen and with household chores. So far, it was a comfortable life with no concern about paying rent or working an eight-to-five job. Helping with her dad was payment enough for her mom, who was grateful her daughter was home.

But the restless, nervous feeling in the pit of her stomach began again in earnest. Although monotonous, her previous job provided a sense of achievement. Now it was time to experience more out of life. Make a difference. Make a name for herself. Do what she liked to do.

That night, Sue got on her computer again and, this time, she searched for "Private Investigator license in New York." The prerequisites for the job required that the applicant be 25 years old, a U.S. citizen, and have a high school diploma. There was also the matter of paying the fee, passing the National Instant Criminal Background Check (NICS), and completing fingerprint verification. Sue had already taken Criminal Justice classes; the only thing lacking was the "official" experience. It sounded like a perfect fit and something easily attainable. Since she was from out of state, Sue also had to check with Monroe County for a New York handgun license.

"Sue Gainer, Private Investigator," she said aloud. The title was exciting. Flopping down on her bed and pillow, Sue started to daydream about it. Maybe she'd even work on a case with Officer Williams. That could prove interesting...

Making up her mind about the officer was more difficult: Did she want to date him or work with him?

"Hmmm," she mulled. *"I may have to think more about this."*

4

The following day, Sue went to the DMV to get a temporary New York State driver's license until the official one arrived in the mail. The next stop was the nearby auto dealership where she picked out a used, black SUV from the lot. The salesman handled the plates at the DMV. Once she had her wheels, Sue filled out the necessary gun permit form, picked up the application for a P.I. license, and crammed a refresher of her Criminal Justice courses. Within a couple of days, she took the training course, which she passed. Her fingerprints went into the system, but it would take a little while for them to clear.

Now, someone experienced in investigating had to lead the way to her goal. Sooner or later, Sue would have to tell her parents about her plans. "Let's get this over with," she whispered to herself one morning, providing the confidence needed to move on.

Her mom was pouring coffee into a mug and walking it over to her dad, who was reading the newspaper.

"Good morning!" Sue greeted with exuberance.

Her mom was immediately suspicious. "Uh-oh. Looks like you're up to something," Carol teased.

Sue sat at the kitchen table, smiling. "I'm going back to work."

Surprised, Carol asked, "Where?" as she placed the coffee on the table and went back for the carafe to fill Sue's cup.

Her dad looked over the top of his paper but didn't comment.

"I'm going to be a private 'eye.'"

"Private 'Eye'? What do you mean? Like a real detective?" her mother asked incredulously with her voice squeaking. "That's so dangerous! Will you have to carry a gun? What if you get shot? I don't want to bury my daughter!" Carol was truly distressed, as the coffee carafe dribbled dark liquid on the clean white linen tablecloth.

Her father grumbled, "Why can't you get a normal job working for corporate America? Or the University of Rochester? Lots of jobs there." Then he turned his attention to Carol, grumbling, "Hey, you're spilling the coffee!"

"Oh!" Immediately, Carol dabbed the stain with a handy paper towel. There was no saving it; the tablecloth would have to be laundered.

They both knew how stubborn Sue could be when she decided on achieving something. She wasn't budging.

"I've already passed the test. It's going to be a while before I take on clients. I need on-the-job training first."

"Where would you do that? Do you know anyone?" her mom asked.

"I have to look into that," she admitted. Sue thought about her work with the Delaware Police and the FBI, but that was another state under strange circumstances. Who would help her in Rochester?

Other investigators, she assumed. She still had research to do.

Jerry, concerned for his daughter's welfare, spoke up with a little anger in his voice and shook the newspaper in his hand. "Do you know what could happen to you? Did you read this article? There's a killer on the canal! They recovered the body of a woman. They haven't found the killer yet. Here, read it!" He handed the crunched-up paper to Sue.

Unfortunately, the news about the body was all over social media and she hated upsetting her dad when he was so sick, but Sue wasn't daunted. It made her think about her own recent experience, however. Could the killer have been right there, watching her? She shook off her fear.

"It's what I'm drawn to do. Don't worry. I'll be alright."

Sue hoped she was right.

5

The social media profile of seventeen-year-old Emily Rogers was filled with selfies, emojis, memes, and gifs, just like most girls her age. Listed were hundreds of "friends," including a few guys she "swiped right" on Tinder but never met in person. There was one particular guy on Tinder who interested her, though. In his profile picture he was shirtless with muscular arms that could easily lift her up over his head, and abs that made her smack her lips. Total catnip!

Her new heartthrob, Rich Landers, was a bit old for her, but she thought, *"Age doesn't matter, really."* He said he was twenty-four, but, like many online users, male and female, he lied about his age. Rich was actually thirty and using a picture of himself on his Tinder account from six years ago. He was looking for some fresh, young ass and he didn't want to discourage girls who were barely "of age." His earlier attempts garnered some success. An eighteen-year-old girl connected with him online, displaying her long, shiny hair over half her face like "Jessica Rabbit." It made his eyebrows raise with interest. However, when he actually met her, "Jessica" was as blind as a bat and her eyes squinted at him all the time. It was very distracting. Not a total loss, though—

Rich took advantage of what she had to offer. He saw her just once; that was enough, then he wanted to move on, and so he did.

At a mere five-foot-three and one-hundred-and-ten pounds, Emily wasn't exactly his type either, with strange-colored hair, piercings in her lip, ears, and belly button, a tattoo, and lots of makeup, but she was willing to do *anything*. He liked that, especially since sexual gratification was his primary goal.

Emily met up with Rich only when it was convenient for him. She suspected he might have a girlfriend, or even a wife, because he was so secretive about everything. He just told her, "I don't like to share things about myself," when asked where he worked, where he lived, and why they couldn't just go to his house for sex. He'd say with a sly grin, "Isn't it more fun, more adventurous, to do it in the park?" She had to agree.

Rich completely trusted her to remain silent about their lovemaking and not "create waves." Emily was a bit wild, which surprised him for being so young. He assumed she was experienced, and she was. They often "sexted" each other—something they both enjoyed since they found it titillating and a great prelude to sex.

Emily wondered how fortunate she was to find Rich. He was just what she wanted in a man— handsome, muscular, sexy, and a guy who was crazy about her. When she was with Rich, she wanted to tell all those jealous bitches "out there" to f-off! He was her man now!

So, on this unusually warm spring day, when Rich texted to ask Emily out, he said he had something special for her.

"Oh?" the teen replied, feeling relaxed and intrigued. Emily forgave him for all his secretiveness and was excited to receive the gift from her new lover. For hours before their date, she dreamed about some nice jewelry or a sexy negligee for a special occasion. Instead, what she got was a strange, pointy woodcarving of a candy kiss. He called it a "box." She was terribly disappointed. Not a jewelry box, that was for sure. This time her response was "Oh," as Emily blankly stared at the odd present.

"Hold this for me; keep it safe in your bedroom," he suggested. "You can think of me when you look at it." He laughed.

She thought it was a joke and waited for the punch line but there was none. "Right," she replied with a forced smile. She shook it to see if it contained a ring or other jewelry, but there was no sound, no rattle, no movement. She looked for a way to open the "box" but didn't see any. *"Very strange,"* she thought. She grimaced but did not want to express her disappointment or what was *really* on her mind. *("What the fuck is this thing?")*

Emily looked at him and debated her next words. *"Best to be safe,"* she assumed. His big, strong arms might be used against her if he became angry. She wasn't stupid enough to piss off a big guy like him.

That night they drove to a remote spot in a county park. After removing every stitch of clothing she had on, he unzipped his pants, exposing a very large organ. The first time Emily saw it, she gasped, fearing it would hurt her, but she had nothing to fear. They explored everything about each other and then had sex several different ways. The night was hot, but they were hotter.

6

Sue's cell phone rang. She didn't recognize the number right away, but it looked familiar. Finally, she pressed the Answer button.

"Sue Gainer?" the male voice asked.

"Yes."

"This is Agent Sturr of the FBI. Remember me?"

Sue gasped. "Of course!" Agent Sturr was involved in the case in Delaware and called in the police to rescue her boss Lauren from a murderer.

"A funny thing," he joked. "Your fingerprints just popped up as part of the application process for a private investigator's license. What's that all about?"

"How did you get involved in that?" Sue questioned him.

"You'd be surprised what we get involved in. So, you want to be a P.I., huh?"

"Yes, I do."

"Well, I'll tell you what...I'll step up the paperwork on your fingerprints and place a call into the Rochester Police Department, who work with P.I.s occasionally, and put a good word in for you. They'll get you the additional training you need. You'll need to follow their protocol. Can't fly by the seat of your pants, you know, or you'll find yourself in trouble. Fast. Now, we don't need that, do we?"

"No, of course not," she agreed.

"Okay, Sue. Wait for a phone call. And, good luck, kid."

"Thanks, Agent Sturr." He hung up, so she ended the call.

"Wow!" Sue said out loud with a smile on her face. "I guess it pays to know somebody."

A few days later there was a text, reporting that her fingerprints had cleared and a confirmation letter would arrive in the mail. Shortly thereafter, Deputy Chief Mulroney in the RPD, who was responsible for the direct police services to the community, called to set up a meeting with Sue.

"Can you come in on Tuesday, say 1 p.m., for a chat? I'll put you in touch with one of the investigators you can shadow—a guy by the name of Lou Perlo. Smart man."

"Sounds good."

"Lou will get you started on training." He filled her in on what to expect.

"Got it." She thanked him for the call and they both hung up.

Things were starting to move quickly! Feeling grateful for a place to live until she could earn some money, Sue considered her finances. Luckily, she had a small severance from her old job, which was enough to get her by for four or five more weeks.

For the next few days, Sue concentrated on her dad's treatments and his well-being at home. Jerry was weak and tired all the time, so they moved a bed downstairs into the dining room. He also felt nauseous after the last treatment and didn't want to eat. But he ate a lot of Jell-O because it went down easy. Jerry already lost his sense of taste along with ten pounds and had to wear suspenders to keep his pants up. Because he was cold all the time, Carol had to buy him a bulky sweater, which was difficult to find locally in stores in late May. Then he started using a cane for extra walking support. For Sue, it was sad to see her dad go downhill before her eyes. The "Golden Years," they call it. Far from it.

* * * * *

On Tuesday, Sue donned a pair of black dress slacks and a white blouse from her old office job. She drove to the City Public Safety Building in downtown Rochester, parked in the dimly lit garage, walked to the nearest entrance, and went up to the third floor. Feeling the eyes of several people working in the area who were curious about her visit, Sue was eventually greeted by Deputy Chief Sean Mulroney, a fit man in his late 50s, in full uniform, who invited her into his office. A quick glance around the department and a deep breath gave Sue a sense of confidence before Mulroney closed the door behind her.

"Good afternoon, Sue. Have a seat. You certainly have some influential friends! I received a call from FBI Agent Sturr who said you were 'dedicated' and 'clever,' and to give you a chance. He also credited you on saving a life! Why don't you tell me about that?"

Sue sat in the leather guest chair and repeated the story. Her boss in Delaware, Lauren, had been in trouble and Sue promised to be her eyes and ears. When she suspected that Lauren was in grave danger, she called Agent Sturr for help. Lauren most likely would have been murdered had she not stepped in.

Mulroney was impressed.

He advised, "You know, being a P.I. is a very dangerous job, and it requires not only cunning, but the same things we look for in a police officer, including integrity, physical fitness and self-defense skills, patience, an understanding of human nature, communication and negotiation skills, and mental agility. The job could take you into high-crime areas, including places where gangs and drug lords are active, but it could also take you into the lives of the rich and famous, and—don't fool yourself—that can be dangerous, too." He concluded, "You have to take it seriously, anticipate the perpetrator's next move, be flexible and aware of your surroundings at all times."

"I understand," Sue nodded as she responded.

"So, here's a little test," he said slyly. Sue perked up. "How many people were outside my door and what can you tell me about them?"

"I saw a sophisticated woman, African American, who may be your secretary, perhaps in her 50s, wearing a wine-colored dress. And there were two white females at desks in their late 20s, and two police officers discussing something, both older men, one with gray hair and the other with salt-and-pepper hair."

"Pretty good. Here's Lou Perlo's card." He handed it to her. "Give him a call if you don't hear from him in the next day or two." Mulroney stood up and walked around to the other side of his desk. He opened the door for Sue, who stood up and started to leave.

"Thank you for taking the time with me today," she said sincerely.

"Good luck," he responded, "and stay safe."

* * * * *

Two days later, Sue met Lou Perlo at a coffee shop on Park Avenue in the city. Lou was sitting at a table with a cup of coffee, watching the door as she walked in. One of the first things Sue recalled from watching TV detective shows was to never have your back to the door in this profession. Look at every face that comes through the door and watch the hands of threatening persons.

Lou was a handsome man in his late 30s—dark hair in a traditional cut, brown eyes, thick eyebrows, clean shaven, well-manicured, and dressed in expensive clothing, although casual—a black tee and lightweight sport coat. She didn't detect any cologne. He smiled a genuine smile and held her hand for a moment when he introduced himself, and she noted a large ruby ring on his right ring finger. His left ring finger was bare. When he did look at her, he seemed to gaze deep into her soul, as though he knew who she was without knowing who she was. Or did he? After all, he was a detective.

Lou got right down to business. He asked some of the same questions that Deputy Chief Mulroney asked, about her experience and skills. He also informed her that a lot of their work is done at night and she had to be flexible with her time. It also required some investigative work in the city's public records as well as online. Photographic skills with a zoom lens were necessary, just as much as handling a gun. She had to become familiar with the laws of the state, how to handle evidence, when to call for reinforcements, have excellent driving skills including knowing all the city streets, and be able to recognize the truth and weed out the lies. In other words, she needed to be a super woman.

"I can do that," Sue said with confidence.

Lou grinned and nodded. "Okay." Then he continued, "I'm willing to give you a chance. We'll get your training started tomorrow morning. You won't learn everything overnight, but I won't let you go out on a case until I think you're ready."

She affirmed with a nod.

He added, "I do have a staff of two assistants. They're worth their weight in gold. One, Kelsey, is a whiz at online research, including the dark web. The other, Monica, is great with faces. She remembers faces on Wanted posters and can recognize people on closed-circuit TV better than anyone I know. They both handle paperwork, including invoicing, payroll, and bank deposits."

"Can't wait to meet them."

"They will also back us up if we need it. For instance, if we need background information, they will look it up. If we need to create a diversion, they will do it. If we need a male, Monica's brother Maxim will help out on a contract basis."

"Sounds good."

"One of the ladies will set you up in payroll. Unfortunately, I can't pay you the first two weeks because it's all training and some people just don't work out, but after that, you'll be paid an hourly wage. You'll have to submit a payroll form every other Thursday before 4 p.m."

"No problem." Sue was hoping that she would "work out" and not have to be let go! "Do you have other investigators on your staff?" she inquired.

"You're it, Baby." He laughed. "Most move on to their own business or get out of the business entirely. Occasionally, they even die on the job."

Their eyes met. Sue made a small gasping sound. "Oh!"

"Just don't end up dead. That would be a real tragedy," he joked half-seriously as he stared into her eyes.

She took the warning to heart.

.

7

Twenty-two-year-old Tristen Phillips fancied himself a magician. His hand movements were so quick, so stealthy, that no one ever figured out his tricks.

Many kids went to the community college and yearned for a job creating video games or teaching school, but they were never Tristen's goals. All his life, the only thing he ever wanted to be was a magician, but his high school teachers, his guidance counselor, and his parents ridiculed his life choice and pushed him into a worthy trade, that of a car mechanic just like his dad. As a result, that was the current source of his income—and a good income it was! He didn't mind working on cars—he loved them—but his hands were always rough and dirty. That was not a good look for a magician. Obviously, a magician has to have smooth, attractive hands for sleight of hand on stage or television. All eyes would be on his hands.

He would watch and re-watch magicians on *America's Got Talent* and tried to be as good and as creative as Shin Lim, who he considered to be the greatest of all magicians in his lifetime. He also noted the poor performances by other magicians and vowed never to make those mistakes.

Every night after his work at the car repair shop, he'd practice magic in his bedroom. Many nights he stayed up until the wee hours of the morning honing his craft, but that did not sit well with his boss, Mr. Sobieski, who often got on his case about being slow. Every job had an expected turnaround time and Tristen never met those expectations. He wished he cared, but he didn't.

"One more time and you're fired!" Mr. Sobieski would threaten. But Tristen was still working, probably because there was no one to take his place.

Over the years, his dad taught him all about cars. It's true, he loved the workings of a vehicle just as much as his dad, and he was good at it and proud of the finished job and the customer satisfaction it provided. But it just wasn't *magic*.

The other problem was that he had fallen in love. Her name was Emily Rogers. In the fall, Emily would be a senior in high school. They met when they were both performing on a Haunted Hayride. When they kissed for the first time, it sealed their new-found love. A few days later, he performed his magic for her and she was mesmerized by his tricks. She laughed and clapped and begged him to tell her how he made the cards disappear in a puff of smoke. But he couldn't tell her. After all, it was magic!

He suspected that his sweet Emily performed her own sleight of hand every time she went into Walmart or the dollar store. She never had any money, but she'd end up with a phone, jewelry, sunglasses, feminine items, and more. He was afraid she'd get caught when he was with her and he'd be the one going to jail. That would never do, as it might forever ruin his career on stage—if he ever had one.

He decided to have it out with Emily. It was his day off and he called her cell phone.

"Yeah," she answered, after spotting his name. "What's up?"

"Can we meet?"

"K. See you in the usual place at the gas station. Ten minutes?"

"K. Later."

They both ended the call.

Tristen drove his dad's truck to Elmgrove Gas and waited for a few minutes. Checking his straight brown hair in the visor mirror, the young man pushed it to one side, looking more like sixteen than twenty-one. The rotating LED lights in the convenience store window could make anyone go crazy in a short amount of time, but soon he saw Emily run across the busy road, dodging a few cars. Her hair was blue today. He never knew what color it was going to be. *"A bit of a witch,"* he mused with a shitty grin. *"Perhaps we could conjure something up together."*

When Emily hopped in his vehicle, they kissed hello. Her lipstick was blue, too. He managed to casually run the back of his hand down the front of her V-neck t-shirt and discovered that she wasn't wearing a bra. The intimate touch triggered a funny but pleasing sensation in his loins.

"What's going on?" the petite girl asked with a smile after being pawed, a gesture Emily thoroughly enjoyed.

The good feelings from moments ago disappeared as the topic became serious. "Look, we gotta talk."

"About what?" she asked curiously.

"Your shoplifting." The magician looked directly into her eyes as though trying to put her under a spell. It didn't work.

Emily immediately went on the defensive.

"Excuse me? You have a job. I don't. It's as simple as that," she argued.

"Do you want to get arrested? You will one of these days!" he challenged.

"Screw you!"

The spell was broken. Immediately, he regretted his attack; it wasn't well thought out. Intending to offer an apology, he leaned over to kiss her again, but was pushed away.

"Stop it!" he whined. "I just want to..."

"*You* stop it! I *hate* you!" Emily cried, not letting him finish his sentence. She tried to open the door.

Shocked at the unexpected response and wanting to control the current frantic situation, Tristen grabbed her shirt, trying to keep her in his truck. "No, Emily, please don't go!" he pleaded. The flimsy fabric of her shirt began to rip.

She stopped and stared at him. "You bastard! Look what you did!" There was a gaping tear in the seam. He stared at it aghast, noting that part of her breast was exposed.

"I didn't mean to!" was his plaintive cry.

"Never call me again!" she ordered as she jumped out and slammed the door shut.

Heartbroken, he watched the love of his life cross the busy road again, clutching her shirt and disappearing down the side street. He wondered, *"Did she mean what she said? Will she forgive me tomorrow? It happened so quickly and now she's gone! I should have been more sensitive with my words, too."*

Grabbing her shirt *was* a very aggressive thing for him to do. *"What if she calls the police? I'll be screwed!"* he suddenly feared.

After a minute or two of sadness and anxiety, Tristen glanced down and saw a few strands of iridescent blue hair on his passenger seat. When he got home, he put those strands in an envelope and sealed it. For now, it was all he had left of Emily, unless...

The young magician started devising a plan in his mind. "Yes! That's what I'm gonna do!" he exclaimed aloud with satisfaction. Tristen smiled to himself; he almost laughed! He decided right then and there that he would use his magic to make her reappear back in his life. He hoped his plan would work.

8

Dan Gilson liked to dabble with carpentry after his release from prison. It was something he learned "in the big house." If you learned a "trade" and didn't cause trouble, chances were that you'd be granted an early release, and that's what happened to Dan.

He didn't like to discuss what got him arrested. If you were a cop, you'd have access to his record; but if you weren't a cop, it was none of your business. Truth be told, Dan was sentenced to 25 years for manslaughter when he was 42 years old, but only served 10 years. His upper lip still twitched when someone—anyone—brought it up. He was still an angry man. The people close to Dan knew not to make him mad, especially after a few shots of whiskey, a crime itself under his probation. Otherwise, strangers viewed him as a hermit-like creature—only going out in public when there was something he needed, particularly at home improvement retailers where he was a regular customer.

Dan also perused Craigslist for specific or unusual items—small, oddly shaped window frames, wood-carving tools, pieces of expensive lumber no one wanted, et cetera. His first major project was building a functional boat in the front yard from scrap wood, attaching a motor, and testing it out on the water. It was satisfying but turning old wood into smaller pieces of fine art was his passion and he made a decent income selling them online. His past was unknown to his customers, and they considered him to be a notable local artist. But Dan did not seek fame; he just needed cash for everyday necessities like food, toilet paper, internet service, and, most importantly, electricity to run his saw.

As a convicted felon, Dan could not own a gun. That didn't mean he couldn't be inventive with his weapons—picture-hanging wire, a wooden stake with a nail in it, or even a screwdriver or wrench. He was always on high alert whenever people were on his property that included an old farmhouse. Dan was a suspicious, paranoid person, due to his time behind bars where only the fittest survived day after day. There was no trust among inmates; their eyes were always moving, always watching the other guy. You had to react fast or it may be your last day on earth.

Today, Dan was reading all the latest Craigslist listings when one caught his eye—a wooden box made from maple and cherry. In the digital photo, it looked like a candy kiss made out of wood. Dan couldn't imagine what he'd do with it, but it intrigued him. He e-mailed the seller who responded right away. Seventy-five dollars was a lot of money to Dan but it looked worth twice the price. He could resell it if he chose. The seller said she'd deliver it. That made Dan a little uncomfortable, but he was always prepared for the unexpected.

It turned out that the seller was a slim, young girl with blue hair, blue nail polish, and blue lipstick. He had to giggle when he saw Emily Rogers for the first time, but she was very serious about selling her carved wooden box.

The thing was, Dan stayed away from women, for the most part. That's what got him in trouble before, when he became jealous and killed a man, and he didn't want a repeat performance in the "pen." But when Emily smiled and got close to his body, it lit a fire inside him, and he began salivating and fantasizing. Perhaps it was her fruity-smelling shampoo, or the interesting body piercings that appealed to him, or just her body heat, but Dan mostly wanted to touch the pure white skin under her clothes. Emily looked like a virgin to him, even though she appeared to have a tough veneer. His lip started twitching as he got closer and closer to her. Momentarily, he put his hand on her upper back where there was a tiny hummingbird tattoo. Emily didn't seem to notice anything was "off"; he seemed like a fatherly sort of man to her. Dan, on the other hand, was highly aroused and he bit his lip to keep it from twitching. But when he thought about forcibly having sex with her, he instantly thought of the possible consequences—prison. It was enough to snap him out of his present state. At least for the moment. Some habits are hard to change.

Seventy-five dollars was counted out and handed to Emily, allowing a brief contact with her long, white fingers. He noticed she wore several silver rings and wondered how much those rings were worth. She caught him staring, so he quickly averted his eyes. Emily thanked him for the money and left.

Dan watched her walk to the bus stop, thinking all the while that he wished he had one night with her. Or even just one hour. He went into his small, run-down house and looked her up on social media. There she was in her profile picture with bright, purple-colored hair this time, and purple nails and lips. Almost all of Emily's pictures were selfies in puckered-kiss poses. He printed out several photos of her on his inkjet printer and started fantasizing about playing with her body, which she freely displayed in some of her posts and which he had the pleasure of touching for a few seconds. He inserted a thumbtack into the corner of each photo and stuck them on the wall over his computer desk.

"Damn, I'm going to hell, for sure," he concluded as he stared at each pose. "But I'm sure going to enjoy the trip! Hahahaha!"

9

The landline telephone rang and Carol answered the cordless handset.

"Sue, it's for you. Someone named Carrie McElroy." Her mother held out the phone.

"Oh! Carrie! From high school! How did she know I was back in town?"

Her mother covered the speaker on the phone and whispered, "Why don't you ask her?"

Sue took the handset from her mother. "Carrie! Hi! How are you?"

Carrie responded on the other end of the call, "I'm great! I drove by your house the other day and saw a U-Haul in the driveway with Delaware plates. I was so excited because I knew you came back! Can't stay away from us, huh?" She laughed.

"Looks like I'll be staying, at least for the time being." Sue explained to Carrie about her father's illness.

"Oh, I'm so sorry to hear it. I'll keep him in my prayers."

"Thank you." Sue changed the subject. "Do you want to get together?"

"How about tomorrow night?" Carrie suggested. "There's a bunch of us doing a bar crawl in the East End."

"Hmmm. Sounds like trouble...but I can't wait!" Sue exclaimed gleefully. They both laughed. They exchanged cell numbers, and Carrie said she would text Sue when she was ready. Sue had something fun to look forward to.

* * * * *

The next morning, Sue promptly showed up in Lou's office. Not plush by any means, but it had a comfortable love seat, walnut end-table, and a modern lamp. There were two young, attractive, casually dressed women at desks whom she assumed to be Monica and Kelsey. A quick glance at their name plates and she knew Kelsey had blonde hair and Monica had dark hair.

"You must be Sue," Kelsey said. "We've been expecting you. Won't you have a seat? Lou will be out shortly."

As Sue sat down, she said, "Yes, thank you. I take it that you are Kelsey. And," looking at the other girl, "you must be Monica. Lou told me all about you." The two girls looked at each other and giggled.

"Did he? You'll get to know us quite well," Monica admitted in a slight Russian accent. "You can always depend on us. We are quite a team!" They giggled again, which made Sue smile.

Kelsey turned to Monica, *sotto vocce,* "Should we invite her?"

Monica whispered back, "Might be fun!"

Kelsey looked at Sue and spoke up, "Monica and I are having a pajama party and sleepover next Friday night. Do you want to come? We're going to watch a James Bond movie."

"Um, I don't want to intrude..."

Unabashed, Kelsey shook her head, her long, blonde hair swishing from left to right, "Nonsense!"

"Well, okay," Sue agreed and smiled.

"Good! I'll write out the address." Within a minute Sue had Kelsey's business card with her address on the back.

"Thanks. That's very nice of you. Should I bring my PJs?"

"Just wear them! No one cares these days what anybody wears. We'll have wine and make popcorn and ice cream sundaes, if you want."

"Oh, okay. I'll bring the ice cream. See you then, if not before," Sue concluded with a smile. It was sweet of them to include her, she thought, and it sounded like fun.

The oak door to Lou's office opened and Lou walked into the waiting area and stood with his hand held out in a welcoming gesture. Sue stood and shook it in a confident manner, then followed him into his office.

"Welcome to our 'base,' as we call it." Lou sat in a tall black leather chair, while Sue sat in a gray-fabric guest chair. He continued, "In a while we'll take a ride to the gun classroom where you'll familiarize yourself with AK-47s and AR-15s to automatic handguns, revolvers, rifles, and shotguns and their ammo. You'll hear names like Glock, Smith & Wesson, Beretta, SIG Sauer, Remington, and others. Eventually, we'll train you to use a taser for non-lethal defense."

Sue interrupted, "I own a Glock 19, and I already contacted the county for a license."

"Perfect!" Lou replied, then continued, "There will be some reading material then you'll need routine target practice. Not everything will happen overnight, of course. By the end of a month or so, you should be ready for your first assignment."

Lou went on to say, "We also need to get you into physical fitness training, including boxing and a certified self-defense class." He looked at her closely. "You appear to be in good shape, but you need to spend at least four hours a week in the gym."

Sue nodded in agreement and glanced at his "build." Even though he wore a sport coat, she could tell he was fit.

"Lastly, you need to completely comprehend the laws in New York—what we can and can't do on the job or to suspects. We'll sign you up for a couple of sessions, but we'll also give you some reading material. You'll need to think on your feet in most circumstances. No alcohol on the job unless it's part of the job."

"Got it," Sue responded.

"Before we go," Lou added, "there's paperwork to be filled out." He handed her a clipboard with a few sheets of paper. "We need a copy of your driver's license and vehicle registration, too. I'll give you a half-hour or so. Just give it to one of the ladies when you're done." The multiple-page form required her Social Security Number, checking account number for direct deposit, and emergency contact. When Sue saw that, she knew this was serious. It was really happening!

She got up and went back into the waiting room to fill out her paperwork. Later, Kelsey showed her their locked equipment room, housing a large, padlocked gun safe, handheld cameras, and an assortment of lenses, body cameras, tiny spy cameras, camera doorbells, voice recorders, laptops, batteries, and even wigs and disguises! Kelsey said, "If there's anything you need but don't see, just ask."

Eyeing all the equipment, she thanked Kelsey. As if timed, Lou came out and asked, "Ready for your gun refresher?"

"Yes," she said simply. The two of them walked out to Lou's car, a silver BMW M3, which rode like it was built for the racetrack. Sue was very impressed.

"Do you use *this* car on surveillance?"

"Depends on the job. We also have a nondescript car, an SUV, and a truck. Monica keeps the keys and can show you where they are kept."

When they arrived at the classroom, Sue was astonished at the lineup of guns! She never knew there were so many! She was introduced to the U.S. Concealed Carry Association certified instructor, a square-chinned, middle-aged man with a brush cut named Rodney Chase. Lou informed her, "We call him 'Sarge' because he used to be a drill instructor in the Marines." Sue thought he looked the part.

"Nice to meet you, Sarge," she said with a smile. His response was simply, "Ma'am." She could tell he was all business.

Sarge started his well-rehearsed spiel. He first went to a shotgun and its shell. Sue got to examine the shell in her hand and to hold the gun. Sarge explained how the shell is filled with gunpowder and sends small projectiles down the barrel when the trigger is pulled. It took two hands to demonstrate the gun due to its size and length. He told her that shotguns were primarily used by hunters, but sometimes used in crimes.

Then Sarge picked up a rifle, another long-barreled gun. He showed Sue how to hold it against her shoulder and fire, again requiring both hands. He explained that this long-gun was used for distance, a favorite of snipers. "A rifle can use several kinds of rounds, including .22 caliber and Remington .223," he explained. He showed her the ammo samples.

"Next are the AR-15s and AK-47s, categorized by some as 'assault rifles.'" Sarge continued, "These weapons are strictly controlled by the government because of the switch that allows shooters to change from semi-auto to full-auto. AR-15s are typically semi-automatic rifles and can hold up to 30 rounds of ammunition, but many states, including New York, restrict the number of rounds allowed. The Remington .223 round is the ammo of choice. The AK-47 is basically the same rifle, but made in Russia and often used in warfare in the Middle East, but also by police here in the U.S."

He finally came to the handguns.

He continued, "I'm sure you've heard of most of these." First, he pointed to a revolver. "This is a Ruger .22 caliber single-action revolver, meaning one shot each time the trigger is pulled. There are several manufacturers of revolvers, named for their revolving chambers." He spun one. "They are thick and a bit heavy, but that doesn't mean they can't do the job. You will get a chance to use one at target practice."

He picked up the next handgun in solid black. "This particular double-action revolver is a Ruger LCR .38 snub nose." He let her hold it. "Double-action means that the trigger performs both the cocking and firing. A little bit harder to find the trigger 'sweet spot' on this model, but it's something you get used to with practice. As you can see, the hammer is encased, for safety reasons. It's not as easy to hit the target with a snub nose, as some gun dealers promote. Takes a lot of practice, but the Ruger LCR is lightweight for carrying in a purse or on an ankle."

He examined the revolver in his hand. "This particular gun features a five-shot capacity." He took the gun and swung the cylinder open to show her how the bullets are loaded and ejected. "Many revolvers today can also hold a bullet in the chamber. That can be deadly when the gun is in the hands of the wrong person."

Moving on to a handgun with a long barrel, he said, "And here's a '.357 Magnum,' not the best for practice or training, but a good self-defense gun. The short-barreled revolvers are better for concealed carry for obvious reasons."

As an afterthought he added, "By the way, revolvers don't leave casings behind as evidence the way other handguns do. The spent casings remain in the cylinder."

Sarge stepped forward to the next group of guns—pistols. "Here we have the most popular gun used by law enforcement, the 9mm. This one's a Glock 19. It's slimmer than a revolver so it's easier to conceal. And it's easy to handle and the recoil is fairly easy to control. It uses a smaller round than other calibers, so you can fit more rounds in the magazine." Once again, she gripped the display gun in her hand and felt the trigger.

Sue informed Sarge, "This is the gun I have."

"Good choice."

He continued, "Other calibers include .380 and .45 Automatic Colt, and the .40 Smith & Wesson. And unlike revolvers, shell casings are ejected from pistols."

Sarge explained, "With semi-automatic handguns, like the SIG Sauer here..." He picked it up. "...you pull the trigger, the gun fires, it cycles itself, and it's ready to fire the next time you pull the trigger. You don't have to do anything else. With full-autos, the gun will continue to fire until you take your finger off the trigger. Most fully automatic handguns are illegal for that reason."

It was a lot to remember, but she was hopeful that all the information would come back to her at target practice.

"Thank you for going over all of this for me. I hope I can remember all of it!" Sue said.

"I'm sure you'll catch on pretty quick," Sarge commented with as much of a smile as he could muster. "I'll see you again at target practice and the next class."

Lou, who had been following the conversation from a few steps away, was now at her side.

"Sarge? Once again, thanks for your time," he concluded. Sarge nodded and walked away.

As they walked out to Lou's car, Sue asked, "What additional things will I learn in the class?"

"Well, you'll learn how to safely load your gun; store it; drop, roll, and shoot; be aware of your target; and clear jams and malfunctions."

"I'm looking forward to it," she said assuredly.

Arriving back at her parents' house, she took a short nap after such an eventful day. There was a fun night ahead of her with Carrie and she wanted to be ready for *anything*.

❧ 10 ❧

arrie's text appeared on Sue's fitness watch—
it was time to pick up Carrie at her house.
When Sue arrived, she was surprised to hear
a child crying and looked around, curious about the
source of the cry. Carrie came to the door with a baby
on her hip.

"Who's this?" Sue asked as she reached out to
soothe the cherub-faced little boy.

"This is Justin, my son. His father is no longer in
the picture."

"Oh, I'm sorry." Sue looked at Carrie, hoping she
would provide her with more information.

"I have full custody. My mother will be here soon
to babysit. Sit down and make yourself at home! I need
to finish feeding him." Carrie went into the kitchen.

Sue sat on a couch alongside a blanket with toys,
an almost-empty baby bottle, and a pacifier. She
looked around the room, which was cluttered with
baby things—a playpen, a riding toy that he could
push with his feet, soft blocks, stuffed animals, a
musical school bus, cloth books, and a colorful cell
phone with big buttons. Sue picked up the cell phone
and pushed a button. It asked, "Do you want to play
with me?" Another button said, "I love you."

The front door opened and Carrie's mother, Judy, stepped in. "Oh, hello, Sue!" she greeted. "Long time no see!"

"I was going to say the same thing to you!" Sue stood and gave her a hug.

Carrie came into the living room with Justin and handed him over to her mom.

"Hello, Big Boy!" Judy kissed him over and over which made him giggle and kick his chubby feet.

Judy turned to the girls, "Now you two have a good time. After Justin goes down for the night, I'm going to go to sleep myself in the guest room." Apparently, she was used to this routine.

"Thanks, Mom," Carrie said as she hugged her. "See you later." She grabbed her small tan purse with a thin shoulder strap and headed out to Sue's car.

It was a 10-minute drive to the East End. Sue gave Carrie the run-down about her training to be a private investigator.

"Wow, that's amazing!" Carrie responded. "I have a gun, too—a Ruger .380 pistol."

"Is it safe to have it in the house with a child?"

"I have to buy a gun safe. Right now, I keep it next to my bed."

Sue didn't like the sound of that. "Are you afraid of living alone?"

"It's not that. I'm afraid of Justin's father."

"Oh!"

"He's furious that he didn't get shared custody of Justin. I don't trust him. Just today we had an argument over the phone."

Not wanting to ask her about the argument, Sue inquired, "Is he allowed to see Justin in your home?"

"No. At least not right now. He's appealing that ruling. He's not 'dangerous' but he's also not a nice guy. I don't want him near my child."

"I'm so sorry," Sue lamented, considering the situation.

After parking the car, they walked to the bar where Carrie was meeting up with her friends. It was dark inside but a noisy Friday-night crowd had already formed. The girls could hear the clinking of glasses and beer bottles and loud music. It was a mixed crowd of all backgrounds and ethnicities, mostly in their 20s. Everyone seemed to be happy, as laughter came from all around. She heard a woman's voice yell, "Carrie! Over here!"

Carrie led Sue to a table for six in the back corner. Sue recognized a couple of the girls from high school. A waitress came over and took their order. Sue asked for a Genny beer on draft. The first few sips went down easy. She said, "It's good to be home," and held up her glass as if in a toast. Someone ordered Buffalo chicken wings, which they devoured in no time.

Excusing herself to wash her hands, Sue was gone for a few minutes, but when she returned to the table, Carrie was gone.

"Have you seen Carrie?" The women looked at her and shrugged. No one knew where she had gone. In fact, no one even missed her. Carrie's purse remained at the base of the chair where she had been sitting.

Sue pushed her way through the crowd and spied Carrie at the bar, talking to a tall, good-looking man with dark hair. She was about to speak to them when she heard the man threaten Carrie.

"You bitch! You're going to be sorry you messed with me!" he scowled. He shoved her and she almost fell backwards, but Sue caught her.

"What's going on here?" Sue interrupted in a commanding voice.

The man ignored Sue, grabbing his money from the bar and heading for the door.

Carrie regained her stance. She looked at Sue with tears in her eyes. "That was Jared Poole, Justin's dad."

Sue watched Jared walk away from the bar, wondering if she should follow him. Not being prepared for a confrontation, she decided not to.

The bar wasn't a good place to discuss personal matters, so Sue asked Carrie if she wanted to leave. There were several people already staring at them.

"Not right now. I'll be okay. I just need another drink." Carrie headed back to the table of girls.

Sue chose not to have another beer; she'd stay sober, just in case. Carrie dried her eyes and ordered a second drink. The rest of the night was rather somber, as Carrie chose to remain silent and immersed in thought. About an hour later when their friends went on to another bar, they decided to head back to Carrie's house.

"What kind of vehicle does Jared have?" Sue asked as she looked ahead toward the public parking lot.

"It's a black pickup truck. That's what we argued about earlier. He wants me to co-sign on a new car loan and I refused. He wasn't very happy with me." Carrie rambled on, "Do you know how much those vehicles cost? I don't want to be responsible for that loan! And why should I be responsible? We're not together anymore. We're not even married!"

Sue stared at the dark truck that had just pulled out of the parking lot, wondering if it had been Jared's.

Carrie also spotted the same vehicle before it disappeared down the road. "He'll find some other sucker," she snarled.

"Was that Jared's truck? It matches your description. I couldn't see who was driving."

"I don't know. He could have gone to another bar." Carrie seemed to dismiss the situation.

They got into Sue's SUV and drove to Carrie's home where they both went inside.

The house was quiet, and they kept their voices down so that her mother and the baby wouldn't wake up. They took their shoes off at the door.

Carrie whispered, "Let me show you my gun." A wave of the hand was meant for Sue to follow.

They crept up the stairs and into her bedroom where they sat on the bed. Carrie opened her bedside table and started to shuffle through some personal items and papers.

"Oh no! Where is it?" she cried softly but excitedly.

"What? The gun?" Sue asked with a sinking feeling.

"It's gone! I KNOW I put it in there. I didn't put it anywhere else!" Carrie was starting to panic.

"Could your mom have moved it someplace safe, like a closet shelf?"

"I never told her about the gun, but I suppose she could have found it. I guess I'll ask her in the morning."

Sue was not liking this at all. "Carrie, if she doesn't know anything about it, you have to call the police to report that it's been stolen."

Ignoring what Sue advised, Carrie looked into her eyes. "I wonder if Jared still has a copy of my house key." Carrie swallowed hard.

That was a very scary thought. "You didn't have the locks changed?" Sue inquired nervously.

"I never got around to it." She paused, then shrieked, "The baby!" She stood then ran to Justin's room. Sue followed.

They looked into the crib and there was Justin, sleeping like an angel. They both breathed a sigh of relief.

Sue could also hear the sound of gentle snoring coming from the guest room. Apparently, her mom, Judy, was fine, as well.

"When was the last time you saw your gun, Carrie?" Sue asked when they were back in Carrie's bedroom.

"Well," the young mom thought. "...probably last weekend."

"Jared could have been here any time between then and tonight," Sue indicated.

Staring into space, they both were worried that he'd come again, and this time he'd have Carrie's gun.

"Tomorrow morning, call a locksmith. And I've got one more thing we might install—a smart doorbell."

"A smart doorbell?"

"One with a surveillance camera. It'll record anyone who comes near your door. Let me handle it."

With that, Sue said goodnight and waited until she heard Carrie turn the deadbolt on her door before she went to her car.

She hoped the deadbolt was enough.

⤜ 11 ⤛

Totally sober, Jared sat in his aging, damaged pickup truck in the bar's parking lot, trying to blow off steam and calm down, but it wasn't working. Carrie infuriated him! After all he did for her, and she couldn't just do this one thing for him? Just co-sign his car loan? He would have to strong-arm his own mother to do it. Then, tonight, when he asked to see his son, Carrie said no to that, too! He banged his fist on the dashboard as he seethed and swore at her. "Fuck you, Carrie! He's MY son! And I will see him whenever I want! I'll show *you!*"

Baby Justin was his own flesh and blood, part of his very essence. However, Jared never considered how much work it takes to raise a child, how much time, attention, and love a child needs, or how much money it costs to provide for this tiny child to grow up and be educated. Jared had no plan. He just wanted what belonged to him.

Thinking back to his own childhood, Jared always felt as if his parents considered him a burden, an unwanted child due to his illness. He had spent many days in the hospital with doctors and nurses poking and prodding him. And when "living" at home, he never had friends like most kids. He'd stare out the window as other kids rode their bikes, played baseball, and went to school every day. That wasn't the life he was given. He felt cheated, and that left him angry.

When he received a gift, usually a book, video games, or music CDs, he'd hide them in his dresser or under the bed so that no one would borrow them and never return them. They were HIS presents, his possessions.

Jared never prayed for a miracle—he didn't believe in them, or God, or guardian angels, or Santa's elves, or any other mystical or magical, make-believe creatures. *"If there is a God, why am I so sick all the time?"* he'd think to himself. *"It's all phony!"*

One day, when he was practically a man, his parents sat him down and explained a new procedure. Unemotional, he asked, "If I die, what happens to my stuff?" His parents laughed but he was filled with consternation. It wasn't funny to Jared.

But then he met Carrie. Carrie, the sweet sixteen-year-old who kept coming to visit him in his later teenage years and throughout his treatments. It seemed she had a thing for him, and Jared liked that. He depended on her to make him comfortable, fill his room with laughter and a bright smile, and bring him little gifts that she bought with her own birthday money.

One summer day, after the procedure which he didn't understand but knew he was feeling better, Carrie provided him a good look at her cleavage, and Jared pulled her to him, madly kissing her. From then on, he wanted it every day, and every day Carrie gave in to his demands without question. She was Jared's girl now.

But it didn't last forever.

Now, tonight, recalling those miserable days of his childhood and teenage years, Jared realized they were now replaced by the miserable days of being an adult. Getting along with people was even tougher than he imagined. It infuriated him when his ideas and demands were ignored or rejected. Plus, Carrie, fed up with his immaturity, no longer doted on him. "You're an adult! Act like one!" she'd say. Angry that she defied him, he said he'd look elsewhere, and he did. He deserved it after the hard life he had.

Sitting alone in the darkened interior of his truck in a crowded parking lot, Jared opened the console, pulling out a small, plastic baggie with an ecstasy pill inside. He popped it in his mouth and washed it down with the bottled water he had in his cup holder. In a few minutes, he started to feel its effects. He relaxed his head against the headrest.

When he started to experience a high, he glanced at his glove box, then reached over and opened it. He put his hand inside, gripping the largest object. He pulled out a gun, looking at it lovingly. It seemed to relax him as he rubbed the barrel, back and forth with his hand, over and over. Then he kissed it.

"Baby, we are going to solve our problems," he said to the gun. He rubbed it on his face and his chest and kissed it again. He put the gun between his legs on the carpet, ready to grab it if he needed it in a hurry. Unzipping his pants, his hand went around his penis, pulling it out, and massaging it, and thinking about what he'd do to Carrie to get back at her for all the times she stood defiant to his wishes, his needs, his demands. It was a sick fantasy, but not to him. He got great satisfaction imagining it; he had it down to a science. He pumped his appendage faster and faster, until he came all over his hand. His head went back against the headrest, as he made muffled sounds of release and satisfaction. No need to attract attention in the public parking lot by voicing his excitement!

After Jared was done, but still feeling a pleasurable high, he cleaned himself up. Jared didn't bother to tuck himself back in. As he worked on the plan in his mind making sure there were no loopholes, he continued to fondle himself. He hated Carrie; she cheated him out of the one thing he really wanted in his life—his son. That's where the gun was going to come in. The weapon gave him a tremendous sense of power and security and it would make Carrie sorry she ever denied him his God-given right. Now, Jared had to take steps to fix that, *no matter what.* Carrie could not win. He had to take his son. He thought sadly, *"Justin may be the only son I ever have."* He knew there may be consequences if he were caught, but life was too short not to take the risk. It was imperative to live with his son while he could. Jail was out of the question, so he had to be smart about this. His plan had to work without any hiccups. He "sort of" had a practice run but it would be much more complicated the second time.

But there was one thing he didn't know about— one thing he hadn't planned for—one thing he hadn't expected.

A private investigator named Sue.

12

It was the wee hours of the night, but Sue could not sleep. Pushing off the bedcover, she stepped onto the soft carpeting toward the small computer desk. The screen lit up as her laptop opened and a dozen icons appeared. After typing in "motion-sensored doorbells," a page popped up listing different makes and models and all their reviews. Security doorbells were very popular and made by many companies but, after researching, Sue chose one that had face recognition and a clear camera. She planned to see Lou in the morning to tell him what was going on with Carrie and her ex and ask if they had any camera doorbells in their storage room. Or, if Lou could not supply one, she might be able to get a "company" discount on a purchase.

When the alarm went off, it was time to leave for her first scheduled training session at the gym. Everything else would have to wait until later.

Her trainer was Tom Gibbs, a muscular man in his early 30s. Tom walked her through the gym explaining all the machines.

"What is your normal exercise routine?" Tom asked.

"I jog the canal for about 45 minutes almost every day," Sue informed him.

"That's great. Did you go this morning?"

"Um, no. I came right here."

"Okay, so I'm going to get you on the treadmill for two miles. You can adjust the speed and incline. Then I want you on the bike for about 15 minutes. Then see me. We'll start out with some easy squats using a seat and see if you're ready for some weightlifting on this machine." He stood before a machine with several weight bars. "I'll give you some instructions so you don't injure yourself."

Sue went through the various exercises, working up a sweat. Tom instructed her on the weight machine and said that they'd gradually increase her weights and introduce her to other machines over the next couple of weeks. After five minutes on the machine, she was done for the day.

Tom added, "We don't want you to do too much on the first day. Let's set you up for regular sessions." They went over to his office and he marked off some days on his calendar and gave her a card with the dates and times. "See you then!" He smiled and moved on to his next appointment.

Back at home, Sue showered and dressed to meet with Lou.

Lou was on the office phone, jotting notes on a pad. She heard him say, "Uh huh, uh huh. Got it. See you in about an hour," before he hung up. She noticed that a different sport coat was on a wooden hanger on the backside of the door and he wore a tight-fitting, navy t-shirt, displaying his tan, muscular arms.

"Morning!" he greeted with a friendly smile. "How's everything going?"

"Good!" Sue explained her gym regimen and said that she was signed up for a self-defense course the following week.

"And how's the boxing coming along?" Lou asked.

"I have a class on Wednesday."

"Excellent. Let me show you where you'll be working when you're in the office." They walked out into the main office area to an empty desk with a personal computer. "Kelsey will get you set up with any office supplies. Is there anything else you need?"

"Well, there is something." Sue paused, thinking how she needed to word the situation. "I have a girlfriend who may have had her gun stolen by someone she knows. I wonder if we can help her out with a security doorbell."

"Unfortunately, she's not a client right now. She *can* be if she gives us a retainer. Or I can recommend a good doorbell, if you need to buy one." Lou wrote down the make and the name of the electronics store and gave it to her. It was the same manufacturer of the doorbell she researched. "Tell them I sent you."

"Thanks, Lou."

Sue didn't know whether Carrie could afford to hire a private investigator, but she would certainly ask. In any case, she planned to call the electronics store and arrange an installation as soon as possible.

* * * * *

The next day Sue gave her mom a much-needed break, sitting with her dad while Carol went to lunch and the movies with her friends. Sue prepared lasagna for dinner and took care of household chores. It was the least she could do for free rent and board.

Jerry sat back in the living room recliner and streamed to watch an episode of *The Untouchables* on the TV.

"Now this is a good show!" he claimed as he sipped from his tall ice water tumbler set in a foam koozie. Sue noticed his voice was cracking up a bit and wondered if it had anything to do with his treatments.

"Dad, how are you feeling?"

"I'm managing."

Concerned that he didn't want to admit to his frailties, Sue stepped up, offering assistance. "You know I'm here to help you. If you want to talk, I'll listen."

He had a tear in his eye, but he was still "the dad."

"Sue, now don't you worry about me. I'll be fine. I know you're an adult, but I still worry about you...carrying a gun and going after bad guys."

"Well, I think most of my cases will be to catch people in criminal acts or get evidence on domestic cases," pointing out that a gun was just for threatening situations, then explaining her training. When Sue looked back at her dad, he was sound asleep, still holding the remote. She gently took it out of his hand, turned down the volume on the TV, and placed the remote on the table. Remaining seated for a moment or two, Sue wondered what the outcome would be for her dad, and if her mom could manage without him, especially as she grew older. She tried to remain positive. That was all she could do.

* * * * *

On Wednesday morning, Sue headed back to the gym, this time to meet with an actual heavyweight "prize fighter"—TiShawn Brown, now retired. He certainly did not look retired to Sue. He was a brute of an African-American man with upper arms bigger than her thighs. TiShawn tied up her boxing gloves and they got right to work.

"Ms. Sue, if you gonna defend yourself, you gotta know how to throw a punch. Just stand next to me for a 'sec' and watch what I do," he instructed in a deep voice.

TiShawn took two quick jabs at an invisible opponent, first with his right, then his left.

"Whatcha gotta do is 'twist your body' to maximize your reach when you punch." The champion boxer showed the maneuver three times—first in slow motion, then two quick jabs. "Now you do it," he said. She demonstrated her version. "C'mon! Twist that body! Jab with your right fist!" He had her repeat it several times until she was comfortable doing it.

"Okay. In this next one, pretend your opponent is prepared for a fight. Lower your torso a little, with your weight on your right leg," He bounced a little on his right leg. "Have your fists up, and take a step forward to your opponent, then step back. A natural step. It's all about balance. Do the same thing if you're pushing to the right, use your left leg. If you're pushing to the left, use your right leg, then go forward, and jab! Bam! Let's see you try it. Use my glove as your opponent."

At first, it seemed a bit awkward, but she got the hang of it, jabbing his glove.

"Okay, you just need to practice that some more. Let's move on to the punching bag. I want you to punch the bag with just your right hand, like this." He demonstrated. "Jab! Bam! Okay, you do it." Sue punched the bag twice. It barely moved.

"Chin down! Twist and stretch that arm!" he ordered. "Jab!" She hit the bag eight more times.

"Okay," he said, "now use your left hand." She switched her stance and punched the bag ten times.

"You got it. Relax. Now I need you to lie on the floor mat and do some leg lifts—just 10 today."

The leg lifts stretched her back muscles and that felt good.

She got up from the mat, ready for the next move.

"Now you're going to punch at my gloves, starting from a squatting position." He showed her how to do it. "Pretend your opponent is going to throw a punch. Be ready with your fists up by your shoulders. Elbows in! Squat to avoid the blow. Lift. Twist, jab right, stretch that arm! Twist! Now left! Squat. Lift. Jab. Bam! Again!" She punched his gloves about 10 times. She could feel the sore muscles in her thighs.

Sue was exhausted and sweaty and hoped she was done, but TiShawn wasn't done.

"One more thing and then you'll be done for today. Heh, heh," he grinned with bright white teeth, although crooked. "So, now I want you to hit the bag using both fists, like this—Bam! Bam! Bam! Bam! 100 times."

Sue gave him "a look," thinking he couldn't be serious, but he was. He counted as she jabbed first with her right, then her left.

"Feel the rhythm, girl! 10, 11, 12..." he counted aloud as Sue continued to hit the bag.

"...97, 98, 99, 100!" he finished at last. "Good job, Ms. Sue. See you next week."

Sue's mouth was so dry, she couldn't speak, so she just smiled weakly and nodded. He helped to remove her gloves and she grabbed a towel and wiped her face. TiShawn chuckled as he sauntered away.

* * * * *

After a shower, fresh clothes, and two much-needed ibuprofen, Sue went to Carrie's to meet the installer for the doorbell. The scheduler at the electronics store had been very accommodating and confirmed delivery and installation within 24 hours.

The installer, Matt, was a nerdy-looking kid about 19 years old.

"Hi, I'm Matt," he said sniffling his nose. "This shouldn't take too long."

He got right to work and not only connected the doorbell, but he also set up the system for viewing activity from inside the house. A small screen was placed on a shelf under Carrie's TV so that all she had to do was glance at it to know who, or what, was near her door. The camera was so good that her neighbors' houses across the road appeared clear.

"Next, I need your phone." Carrie retrieved it from her purse.

Matt downloaded an app and instructed Carrie how to use it so she could view the doorbell camera wherever she went. The girls took turns standing by the doorway to see just how good the camera was with people's faces. They were both impressed. Carrie could also have the app send her a notification if the camera was triggered by movement near her front door. It was quite the system!

He told Carrie, "You might want to install interior cameras as well, if you're worried about break-ins."

Carrie looked at Sue. "We'll talk about it. Thanks."

After Matt was paid, they watched him get into his van through the eye of the camera.

"Neat!" Carrie exclaimed. "But I hope I never see anyone at my door except the mailman."

Afterwards, they sat down at the kitchen table and had a cup of coffee.

"So, did your mother know about the gun?" Sue inquired.

"No," Carrie replied with a distant look in her eyes. She was thinking about her ex and what that meant.

"You really need to call the police and report it stolen."

Carrie looked at Sue. "I can't. It was unregistered."

"Oh! Where did you get it, then?"

"I bought it off the street."

"That's not good. I hope it wasn't used in a crime!" Sue was clearly worried.

As they sat in silence, they both knew, chances were, it probably was.

13

That night, Carrie stood in front of her bedroom mirror brushing her hair. She wasn't really concentrating on it; her mind had wandered to her earlier life with Jared.

A teenage crush. That's what it was. The handsome boy, who had been recuperating after a long illness, was anxious to rejoin the human race. Carrie stood by him during that long year and was grateful that her prayers had finally been answered. He was alive, feeling good, and attracted to her. Before long, they expressed their love for each other in Carrie's bed one cold December night.

In February she took a pregnancy test and it was "positive." Jared was over the moon that he was going to have a child, as chances were slim with his low sperm count. But there it was, a "YES" on the test stick.

Carrie began to plan a life with Jared and the baby. With her meager salary as a makeup artist at a department store at the mall and help from her parents, she bought a tiny bungalow and decorated the second bedroom with all the necessities and imaginative items for the newborn. Strangely, Jared did not want to move in with her. She assumed that perhaps he was planning a proposal and was looking for a larger home for the three of them. She patiently waited, but it never happened.

Jared was not pleased with the shape of Carrie's blossoming body and found himself drawn to attractive, shapely women. In May of that year, Carrie found out through a friend that Jared was seeing a slim, blonde girl, barely 18. Although hurt, Carrie was determined to give their baby the best life possible.

Jared's romance didn't last. Just before the baby was born, he returned to Carrie.

Appearing vulnerable and apologetic, Jared stood in her doorway. "Carrie, I'm sorry. I'm SO sorry. I never meant to hurt you. Will you hear me out?"

Staring at his contrite face, the mother-to-be gave in. "Come in," she reluctantly offered, opening the door wide enough for him to enter.

They both went into the living room and sat down on a loveseat next to each other.

"Carrie, I got scared. I'm sorry I saw someone else. You're the only girl I ever dated. I had to find out for myself what life was like. It turns out that you are the only one I want. I *need* you."

Jared leaned over and kissed her gently on the lips. He tasted her tears and put his arm around her as she sobbed into his chest.

She took him back. Things were almost the way they had been in their dating days. Making love was a bit more challenging, but they were both gratified. With a light heart and returned confidence, Carrie started making plans for the three of them—again.

Justin arrived on a warm September day. Carrie's days were soon filled with breastfeeding, diaper changing, and laundry. Oftentimes, the new mom was exhausted and needed to nap when the baby napped. She expected Jared to help out when there was shopping to do or chores. Carrie retrieved an envelope of cash from her dresser and handed over enough money to him to cover any expenses. He didn't mind helping with chores at first, until he began to feel more like a servant than a lover. There was no time or energy for Carrie to pamper Jared and it was starting to get to him. His mood eventually turned surly and impatient once again.

And then, one day, as Carrie was paying bills, she brought up a difficult subject.

"Money is getting a little tight since I'm not working. Do you think you could pay the hospital bill?"

Irritated, he shouted, "The hospital bill? That's your bill!"

"Well, how about the mortgage payment this month—you've been living here for three months without chipping in."

Raising his voice a notch, he confronted her. "Look, Carrie, do you want me here or not?"

"Well, of course, I want you here, but you've been sitting on your ass, eating my groceries, sleeping in my bed, and essentially freeloading!" she accused. "It's about time you supported me and your son!"

No woman was going to talk to him like that! He hit her face hard enough to give her a black eye. In shock and pain, Carrie didn't call the police but that was the end of their relationship.

"Get out and don't come back," she warned him as she covered her eye with her hand. He got up to leave. "Don't let the door hit you in the ass!" Carrie yelled as he walked out, hoping it would hit him good and hard. That's what he deserved.

Then alone, Carrie wept. The tears were for the dreams she had, now shattered, and the fear that Jared might return and do them more harm.

Today, as she looked into the mirror and at the shadows of her past, she remained fearful for herself and little Justin, who was so innocent and trusting. Carrie knew that Jared could not be alone with Justin, even for a second. If Carrie had to work or go to an appointment, she called her mother and asked her to watch Justin. The rule was, don't answer the door, don't let anyone in, not even the meter reader.

Jared kept insisting on seeing his son and being a part of his life, but Carrie would not allow it and that incensed Jared. She thought about moving, but she was sure that Jared would follow her mother and eventually find them. They were at risk as long as Jared was out there.

So, Carrie bought a gun. It was not easy to obtain, but a friend of a friend of a friend got it for her, bought some ammo, and delivered everything to her house. Although she had never handled a gun, much less fired one, she could aim and pull the trigger. That's all she needed to know. It was kept in her bedside table, giving her some peace of mind.

Did she ever sleep well? No. Carrie imagined that Jared enjoyed the thought of frightening her without even being there. It gave him power over her that she couldn't deny. But she had power, too. She had Justin.

When Carrie saw that Sue had come back into town, there was a sense of relief. Sue had always been a good friend when you needed one, a person you could rely on in difficult times, or times like this when an angry ex was out there.

Justin began crying in his crib. It was time to feed him. Putting down her hairbrush and going to his room, she spied the chubby baby holding onto the crib railing, with his little legs shaking from his own weight. He had pulled himself up for the first time. Something Jared would never see, never be a part of.

"Did you have a nice nap, Justin? You did? Do you want something to eat now?" Carrie purred. Justin tried to jump up and down with happiness but lost his balance and fell on his bottom onto the mattress. "Haha. Good try, Justin! See! You're getting stronger every day!" She picked him up and gave him a big kiss. As she carried him downstairs, she thought, *"If Jared thinks he will ever have custody of Justin, it will be over my dead body."*

14

Dan had been doing a lot of thinking lately, mostly about Emily. The photos of the little temptress hanging above his computer desk were a constant tease. Obsessing about her wasn't good enough; it was time to make something happen. Perhaps it would be mutual; maybe she had been thinking about him as well.

He called her cell.

"Hey, Emily, this is Dan. Remember me? I'm the guy who bought the wooden box from you."

"Oh, yeah," she replied. "What's up?"

Dan's fears diminished. *"At least she didn't hang up!"* he thought.

"I'm wondering if you could stop by again. I've been trying to open the box but it's the darnedest thing! I figured you could show me how to do it."

She hesitated. "Well, I never opened it myself."

Dan would not take no for an answer. "You young people have a mind for puzzles and games, and between you and me, maybe we can get this thing open."

"Well," she said still considering it. "I'd have to take the bus."

"I'd hate to have you do that. Can I pick you up somewhere?"

"Sure. How about Elmgrove Gas? It has crazy lights in the window. It's across from an auto repair shop."

"I know where that is. When?"

"About an hour?"

"Alright. Bye." They disconnected the call.

Dan went to clean himself up, smiling and excited about the prospect of being with this young, sexy girl.

Emily thought, *"Ugh. This is not what I wanted to do, but maybe it will only take a few minutes."*

* * * * *

Emily Rogers left home wearing a tank top with colorful butterflies on the front, cut-off jean shorts with fringe, and a large black leather bag slung over her shoulder. The blue of her hair was iridescent in the sunlight. As she walked out, she could hear her mother yell, "Don't slam the door!" but she did it anyway. It was a joke between them and Emily chuckled at the thought of it. They often teased each other because they knew each other so well.

Despite Tristen's original plan to use magic to bring Emily back, he had been texting her every half hour, but she refused to respond. She was still mad at him for ripping her shirt. That was not cool.

Now, as Emily walked down her driveway, there he was, parked at the curb in his dad's pickup truck. Irritated, Emily thought, *"If he works on cars all the time, you'd think he'd buy his own damn car!"*

Tristen was saving up for his own vehicle but the monthly payments were just too high.

He got out of the truck and walked up to Emily.

"What do you want, Tristen? I thought I told you not to bother me anymore!"

"Emily, I want to apologize for everything. I shouldn't have said what I did, and I shouldn't have put my hand on you or rip your shirt. I was being a jerk."

Emily liked Tristen, but he was like a brother or a friend, not a lover. His kisses did not excite her; in fact, they were rather childlike. She wanted a man! Why waste her time on a "kid," even if he was twenty-one?

"It's over between us, Tristen. I've moved on."

"What do you mean you've moved on?" he asked nervously.

"I'm seeing someone else."

Tristen was stunned. Emily, the girl he loved, the woman he wanted to be with for the rest of his life, was seeing someone else! Hearing her words was like a sword through his heart. His first reaction was to plead for her and cry, but she shut him down.

"Leave, Tristen. And don't come back." Those were her final words to him, as she turned her back on him and walked down her street toward the main highway.

Tristen felt rage for the first time in his life, not directed at Emily, but at the man who dared to take his sweet girl from him. All the pain and anguish was too much to bear. Jealousy, fear, and anger took over his brain and he wasn't thinking rationally. He had to find out whom she was seeing. His primary objective was to get her back, *no matter what*. Now, Tristen needed to follow her to see if she was meeting up with this other guy.

* * * * *

Dan arrived at the convenience store/gas station a little early, parking in front of the door. He went inside and bought a pack of cigarettes from a guy who spoke broken English. Without being too conspicuous, he checked out where all the surveillance cameras were, then went back to his truck. He drove to a nearby donut shop and turned around, returning to the gas station, this time parking around the corner of the building where there weren't any cameras.

He watched as Emily ran across the road, holding her black bag. He noticed the teen's cute breasts bouncing in her little tank top. He waved to her, signaling where his truck was parked, and she came right over. She got inside Dan's truck.

Emily said with a little irritation in her voice, "Y'know, you could have brought the box with you. It would have saved a lot of time!"

"Oh! You're so smart! Why didn't I think of that?" Dan responded with a deceptive smile. He had shaved and trimmed his hair and dressed in his cleanest pair of blue jeans and crisp plaid shirt just for Emily, even though his belly hung over his large, metal belt buckle. Dan even dabbed a little aftershave on his face, hoping this pretty young thing might be attracted to him.

* * * * *

Tristen was shocked when he saw Emily get into the truck with some old guy. The man had to be three times her age! The jealous lover followed them at a distance, until the guy pulled into a long driveway that went back to a ramshackle farmhouse with a wooden boat mounted on a trailer sitting in the yard.

He couldn't pull in the driveway without being seen, so Tristen made a U-turn and parked down the road a bit, waiting for them to leave.

* * * * *

Emily jumped out of Dan's truck and walked into the open garage.

"Where is it?" She looked at the empty spot where the box had been placed on her last visit.

"Oh, oh. Come on in. It's inside now."

She followed him in, noting everything about the house and the lack of upkeep.

He led her to his same-floor bedroom. "Ah, there it is! On my dresser!" he pointed out.

She walked over to get it, as he quietly closed the door and turned the lock on the knob.

"Well, it must have a trigger latch for it to open," she said as her hands searched for it.

"Yes, a trigger. I knew you might know about this stuff!"

She continued to look for the latch, as he calmly walked up next to her.

"Can I help?" he asked, now so close he could smell her again. His lip started twitching.

"Mmm, no. It might just take a few more minutes, but I'll figure it out," she replied as she concentrated on the task at hand.

Dan could wait no more. He put his hands under her tank top and grabbed her breasts from behind. He pulled her close and started kissing her neck, just above the hummingbird tattoo.

Emily dropped the box on the bed and tried to flee, but Dan was very strong and he held her body tightly, cornering her between the bed, the dresser, and the back wall. Feeling her tender white skin, her breasts, and her body with his rough hands was orgasmic. If only she'd stop fighting and enjoy it as much as he was!

"No!" she yelled, as she kicked and tried to release herself from his grip.

Emily tried to climb over the bed, but Dan grabbed her leg and pulled her back. That's when she kicked him solidly in the groin.

"Eee-ahh!" he cried out in pain.

To protect his groin from further assault, he let go of her leg. Dan bent over, gasping. His exhale sounded like a wounded dog.

Emily successfully jumped over the bed, leaving behind a few strands of blue hair and a tube of lipstick that rolled out of her bag. She unlocked the door and opened it, ran through the rest of the house then outside and down the street as fast as she could.

Her heart beating wildly, Emily didn't know if he'd try to follow her, so she ran past the bus stop and kept going. When she reached a burger joint, she went inside and into the Ladies room. Locking herself in the stall, Emily stayed there until her breath slowed. After checking to make sure her cell phone was still in her back pocket, Emily pulled it out and sent an urgent text to the one person she trusted.

* * * * *

Tristen saw Emily running down the long driveway to the road. She never glanced his way but kept running.

"Something bad must have happened!" he realized. He followed her for a few blocks to see where she'd go. When she went inside the Burger Barn, Tristen pulled in and parked on the far side of the building so that he could see if she was being followed by the old guy. As far as he could tell, she was not. Not yet, anyway.

* * * * *

Rich saw the text from Emily. "Rich, pick me up at the Burger Barn NOW."

He wondered what was up. Rich took his time driving there as he couldn't imagine what was so important. *"Is her burger getting cold?"* he thought, assuming that Emily was just being a teenage drama queen.

Twenty minutes later Rich arrived at the Burger Barn. Emily was watching for him, but she was frightened when a few similar-looking black pickup trucks pulled into the parking lot during her wait. One could have been creepy Dan Gilson's. She tried to stay hidden, as she peered out carefully from under a large window advertisement.

Rich came inside and saw Emily still peering out the window. "What's up?" he asked.

Startled, she turned around, gasping. Once she recognized Rich and relaxed, Emily angrily shouted, "You scared the shit out of me!"

"What's going on?"

When she caught her breath, she continued, "It's a long story. Look. I gotta go to Walmart. I lost my lipstick. I'll tell you the whole story when we get there." Emily felt safe at last in Rich's truck. She unwrapped a stick of blue gum and put it in her mouth and slouched down in Rich's passenger seat.

Rich looked at her smeared blue lipstick, which, at one time, matched the iridescent blue of her hair. He just shook his head, not understanding the calamity of it all. "You dragged me out for that? It better be worth it," he snickered.

"It will. I promise."

* * * * *

It was quiet. Very quiet, for the first twenty minutes in the parking lot of the Burger Barn. Finally, Tristen saw a black pickup truck pull in—it was a mature man, but certainly not the old man he had seen her with. He wasn't aware of any connection between Emily and this guy, but a few minutes later, Emily jumped in his truck and they took off.

Tristen pulled out of his parking spot and followed the truck for miles.

"Where the heck are they going?" he asked aloud to himself.

* * * * *

As Rich and Emily drove to Walmart, she revealed a secret to him. "I have a surprise for you. For us, actually."

"Oh yeah? Like what?" he asked with piqued interest.

"Walmart first," she ordered, sitting up straight in her seat now that the threat was gone.

They arrived within a few minutes and he parked near the exit door of the big-box store. She jumped out while Rich remained in his car, waiting for her to return.

About ten minutes went by, and Rich was getting anxious. *"Where is she?"* he whispered under his breath.

Finally, he spotted her walking towards his truck, spitting out her gum, leaving a sticky blob of blue on the pavement.

"Got your precious lipstick?" he teased.

"I did!" She opened the silver tube, raised the lipstick, and applied the royal blue color to her lips. "And look what else I got! Earbuds for my phone! I swiped 'em," she admitted as she pulled a white package out of her purse.

They were the less expensive kind with wires, typically displayed in the check-out line.

"Oh great. Anyone see you do it?"

"Nah. Do you see security running after me? I know how to do it," Emily pouted. She put the package back in her purse.

"Okay. So what's your surprise?" he queried.

"Let's park somewhere."

Rich took her to the back of the lot, where Emily demanded a kiss first. He complied. One thing led to another. He pushed up her bra and started to fondle her. She unzipped his jeans and reached in, exposing his remarkable manhood. Rich unbuckled his belt and opened his pants further to make things easier. Pushing her head down into his crotch, she did what she was expected to do.

* * * * *

From a safe distance, Tristen kept an eye on the truck Emily arrived in. Eventually he moved from the store entrance, where he saw Emily go in and then out the exit door, to the far end of the lot. He thought that Emily and this guy were going to leave, but instead they parked again in an empty area of the lot. When he saw her head go down and not come back up right away, Tristen was shocked and angry. He knew what was going on! How could she do this to him? Wiping tears from his cheeks, he felt defeated, heartbroken, and hurt. The young man was furious, too, wanting to face her and scream at her, maybe even fight the guy— if they were even a close match, which they weren't. The guy looked strong and perhaps weighed 200 pounds; Tristen was a skinny twenty-one-year-old. Disgusted, he considered leaving but, at the last minute, decided to wait to see what happened next. Perhaps he'd still get his opportunity to have it out with Emily.

* * * * *

"Okay," Rich said coolly, "What's the big secret?"

Emily casually wiped her mouth with her hand. Once again, her lipstick was ruined. "You know that ugly wooden box you gave me a couple weeks ago?"

"Ugly?" His brows furrowed.

"I sold it. Got 75 dollars for it! Maybe we can get a room for a change. Whaddya think?"

The news clearly startled him and she saw it in his eyes. "Don't worry. I'll share the money with you."

Rich banged his fist on the dashboard. "You fool! That wasn't yours to sell!" he yelled, then glanced around in the busy parking lot to see if anyone was looking at them.

"What?" Emily was shocked at his sudden outburst. "Um, I thought you gave it to me. Like a gift."

"I gave it to you to *hold* for me!" The anger Rich was feeling was starting to make his face red.

"Well, I-I... It was just an ugly box." The petite teen started to tremble, upset about her mistake.

"How could you be so stupid?" he accused. He tried to think about how he might recover what he lost.

"I thought you'd be pleased!" Emily exclaimed.

Rich composed himself. "Who did you sell it to?" he asked quietly but firmly, trying to glean the information.

"An old guy named Dan Gilson. Don't ask me to get it back. I'm never going there again! He grabbed my boobs! The pervert!" Emily kept waiting for Rich to express some anger or jealousy that some guy just molested her, but there was no reaction.

"You gotta get it back," he told her coldly.

"I just told you. No!"

He started his truck and, in a fit, drove out of the lot recklessly.

"Where are we going?" she asked.

"For a walk. I need some fresh air."

"A walk? What do you mean—a walk? Who goes for a walk?" her voice raised in anxiety.

"Shut up and just do what you're told."

Emily sat back in her seat, pouting. She didn't like being talked to like a little kid. She started to twirl her hair around her index finger, so tightly that a few strands of dyed blue hair snapped and drifted, ever so lightly, onto the fabric seat of the truck.

After a minute or two, Emily opened the plastic container of earbuds and stretched out the wires, putting them around her neck and laying the buds on her shoulders.

They got on the expressway and drove south a few exits before he turned off into a parking area along the Erie Canal and headed for the trail. The Canalway Trail was surprisingly quiet, perhaps because it was rather late in the day. A few bicyclists zipped by them, as if the couple didn't exist.

Emily put the earbuds in her ears and connected them to her phone. After tapping an app on the screen and choosing a playlist, she was enjoying her favorite rap music as she walked with her boyfriend on one side and the canal on the other. Now, there were no others on the trail and no boats—not that she expected to see any.

Her lover had his hands in his pockets, not because he was chilly or nervous, but to hide his clenched fists which accompanied the anger he felt in his throat. Rich pondered what he should do. That was no ordinary wooden box he had given Emily to keep for him. It had a secret compartment that required know-how to open. And what he placed in that compartment could send him to prison if it fell into the wrong hands. He couldn't have that. Giving it to Emily was supposed to safeguard it since she would never figure out how to open it and it would not be in his possession if the police came calling. But he knew where to find it if he needed it. At least he *thought* he knew where to find it.

Now it was gone. Just like that.

Full of fear and anger, Rich knew it was going to be a major problem to get the box back. He'd have to convince the guy to sell it back, or perhaps the easiest thing to do was to *steal it* back. What if it was too late? What if that Gilson-guy figured it out and opened the compartment? Gilson would contact Emily and she would say that she got it from him. That made him nervous. Very nervous.

* * * * *

Meanwhile, Tristen realized that he could not follow Emily and the well-built man on the canal path right away without being recognized, so he continued to watch and wait from the seat of his truck, which he parked in the public lot a good distance away from the other vehicles. He was ready to make his move when the time was right.

* * * * *

Dan, being a stealthy fellow, knew how *not* to be seen. He had hung back in traffic, with eyes glued to the vehicle which had picked up Emily at the Burger Barn. He was also familiar with the canal path and how to cut through without walking the pavement. His groin still burned, his lip twitched uncontrollably, and he remained angry and wanting revenge. "*A little accident perhaps,*" he considered. Afterwards, he could slip away like a ghost.

He got out of his pickup truck and ducked into the bushes.

15

Twenty-four-year-old Christy Duggins held onto her cell phone, expecting Rich to call, but he never did. Her girlfriends, a bunch of nosey bitches, advised her to get rid of him. According to them, he was "a no-good cheater" and didn't care a rat's ass about the blonde-haired beauty. Recent events made her wonder if they were right. One of her friends, Tonya, claimed that she had seen another woman in the truck with Rich a few days earlier. Of course, there could have been a reasonable explanation. Perhaps she was a sister, cousin, or just someone he knew who needed a ride. Unfortunately, Christy was not a "reasonable" woman, so she was getting more and more agitated.

She knew Rich used drugs once in a while, but didn't everyone? It wasn't like he was an addict; he just used when he was stressed. Perhaps the person in the truck might have provided him with a "little something" and meant nothing more to him.

Then again, why hadn't he called in a week or more? Did he no longer desire her? Were they done? Thinking back over the last few weeks, Rich did seem distant, like he had something on his mind (another woman, perhaps?) but he didn't want to talk about it. He wasn't "a talker" to begin with. Everything about his life was vague. When she asked him outright if there was someone else, he ignored her.

Rich came into her life on New Year's Eve. They met at a restaurant packed so thick with patrons, Christy found it difficult to get to the bar. Once there, the handsome man next to her offered his bar stool and paid for her drink, and they spent the rest of the evening together, watching the ball come down and kissing at the stroke of midnight. It was love at first sight for her. Here was a handsome, single guy, and romantic as well. They danced until 2 a.m. when the bar closed and he went back to her place and stayed the night, making love to her until almost dawn. Then they slept, waking long enough to have "a hair of the dog" cocktail, some cheese and crackers, and another round of lovemaking. Finally, they took a shower together and he bid farewell for the day, as he wasn't feeling very well. Her bed was littered with confetti that had fallen from their hair. She took a photo of it as a reminder of that special night.

The calls and texts from Rich began pouring in several times a day. He was thinking of her, desiring her body, and wanting photos, which she willingly sent. Their passions were raging and everything was "right" with the world for Christy. At least, then.

Now, five months later, it was a different story. Her texts were left unanswered; her calls went to voicemail. In Christy's last effort to call, the recording said the number was unavailable. "*What the heck?*" she thought.

She wanted to drive to his home and have it out with him, then realized she didn't even have his address since he was always at her place.

Rich was a mystery. Who was he, anyway? She did a search on various social media apps. What she saw shocked her. He had a profile on Tinder. That could only mean one thing—he was on the prowl. And she had just been dumped.

That didn't sit well with Christy. Many girls would beg a man to come back—plead, beg, cry that they couldn't live without the guy. But Rich hadn't even given Christy so much as a goodbye or a chance to stand up for herself or an opportunity to chew him out. And, at the moment, there was a lot she wanted to say! What about all those times he told her that he loved her, he wanted her, he needed her, and said he would never use her or leave her? Were they all lies? Of course they were! Christy not only felt "taken," she felt rejected and abused. What excuses would he have? What new lies would he tell? It was all B.S. as far as she was concerned.

Nevertheless, there was an angry curiosity about Rich's new love interest—what did she have that Christy didn't? Then there was the revenge she considered for treating her so rudely. And she was jealous, too. A lethal combination. Hot-blooded Christy was not the kind of girl who sat back and did nothing. Instead, she'd fight—pull hair, scratch a face, bite, and kick—like a tigress on the attack.

The next day, Christy called Tonya. "Hey, it's me. You hafta help me with something."

"Sure! Just don't ask me to rob a bank!" Tonya kidded.

"Remember when you saw Rich with some other bitch?"

"Yeah."

"I need you to go back and see if his truck shows up there again."

"I know what it looks like. I'll see if I can find it. What do you want me to do if I find it?"

"Text me, and I'll meet you there as soon as I can. Keep an eye on it."

"Got it." Tonya packed up a small lunch and coffee and went to the Walmart parking lot where she last saw Rich.

Time went by slowly, but Tonya listened to satellite radio until they started repeating the same music. She had just changed the station when Rich's truck pulled into the lot with the same blue-haired girl she had seen him with before. He dropped her off at the door, then parked.

"Oh my god, it's him!" She called Christy. About a half hour later, Christy pulled alongside of Tonya's car. Tonya pointed out the truck, which had moved to the back of the lot and had been there a while. Christy pulled out a pair of binoculars and focused on the truck. A girl just popped up in her seat. She noted her brilliant blue hair.

"Bastard! Whore!" Christy yelled out. She was infuriated, jealous, and hurt by what she had just witnessed. She wanted to kill her. Or him. Or both!

Rich started the truck and headed out of the lot.

Christy followed. On one occasion, a black pickup truck cut her off, but she could still see Rich's truck ahead. Nothing would give her more pleasure than to see his vehicle go into a ditch on the side of the road with the two occupants inside. With great hostility, she continued to follow them, on and off the expressway, until they pulled into the canal parking lot on South Clinton. While they were on the trail, she hoped to confront him.

"Fuck him!" she said with her teeth and fists clenched. "I'm having it out with him. Right now!" Ignoring a couple of strangers in the parking area, she got out of the car and followed the couple. Twice she had to hide behind a shrub when she saw Rich look back over his shoulder. She was quite sure he hadn't seen her. They were still ahead, walking rather briskly. He had his hands in his pockets; the blue-haired girl had her phone in her hand with a white wire to her ears. He then put his arm around the girl's shoulder.

What she witnessed next turned her hot blood to stone cold. Christy was no longer interested in revenge or victory. She was terrified and started to tremble uncontrollably. She ducked behind two bushes, crouched down, tried to control her breathing, and stayed there until the coast was clear.

16

On Thursday Lou picked up a sheet of paper from his desk and looked at Sue who was sitting across from him. "We have a missing person's case," he informed the investigator-in-training. "Seventeen-year-old girl from Gates, Emily Rogers. Her mother believes she disappeared 24 hours ago but may still be in the area." Lou showed Sue a picture from her social media page. "She has several piercings—ears, bellybutton, and left side of her upper lip—and, when last seen, had blue hair. She's five foot three, 110 pounds."

"Oh no! Not another girl! Is there anything you want me to do?" Sue asked.

"We don't know if there's a connection between the two girls, but we have to keep that in mind. I'll take the lead on this one but I may have you tag along. Take notes. Kelsey's going to check with the local hospitals."

Sue hoped that Emily was just a runaway.

Lou stood. "Let's go visit Emily's mother."

They went in Lou's car and drove to a modest post-World War II home in Gates. It needed painting. Emily's mom opened the worn-out white screen door inviting them inside. She closed it carefully so that it wouldn't bang.

"Come in," she said. She led them to a small living room with an orange-and-brown sofa that looked like it came from the 1980s. There was a small flat-screen TV on a wooden cabinet made for stereo equipment.

"May I get you some coffee?" she asked.

"Not for me," Lou replied.

Sue also passed. "No, thanks."

"What can you tell us about Emily, Mrs. Rogers?"

"Emily left here yesterday about 2 p.m., wearing shorts, a colorful tank top, and black sandals. Her hair was dyed blue, but she changes the color every couple of weeks. She has pierced ears and small rings on her lip and bellybutton. I hate those things, but you know teenagers! And three silver rings on each hand."

"Any tattoos?

"Oh, yes. A small hummingbird, I think, on her upper back. Or is it a butterfly? No, hummingbird!"

"How about boyfriends?"

"Well, I think she's dating a few boys. One's a magician."

Lou seemed startled. "A magician?"

"He's just a young man. Works for his dad at the auto repair shop on Lyell."

He noted that. "How about a best friend?"

"She doesn't seem to mention any girlfriends. Nobody ever comes here."

"Did she say where she was going?"

"No, but it did seem unexpected."

"Why is that?"

"She got a text and she seemed frustrated."

"What's her cell phone number?"

She gave it to him. "585-730-5555. I tried to call but there's no answer."

"Okay, Mrs. Rogers. We'll get right to work on this." They got up and left.

In the car, Lou told Sue, "I'll have Kelsey find out if the police have requested her cell phone records. That might take a few days, but they may get a ping from a cell tower."

"Is there anything else you want me to do?"

"I submitted some paperwork today to speed up your Conceal Carry permit. You should have it soon. Just keep up with your training."

"I have the gun refresher course this afternoon."

He nodded in satisfaction. "I'll call you when I need you." He paused. "Or you can call me if you're onto something."

17

The next day, Sue concentrated on her reading material from the gun class, then, in the afternoon, she had another boxing session. This time TiShawn had Sue work on "hooks" and "upper cuts."

"Okay, Ms. Sue. You ready?" Sue nodded. "This is a left hook. Watch me. My stance is the same as what we used last time for punching the bag. Feet apart. You're going to put the weight on your left foot, twist your body to your right, pivot your heels..." TiShawn showed the move in slow motion. "...and then a quick jab to your right. Bam! He'll never see it coming!"

He continued, "My elbows are at my waist, my fists are toward my body, thumb up. Here it is again. Sharp jab with your left fist! Bam!"

"Got it. Let me try." She bent slightly.

"Whoa! Keep that body straight! If you go 'low,' your punch won't have the same power and your opponent might hit you." She straightened up. "Good," he said, "Now punch!"

"Bam!" Sue tried it a few times with the left hand then the right.

"You got it! Okay, now I'm going to show you an uppercut from the right. It's the same body mechanics as the hook except the punch is coming from the bottom. Shift your weight just a little to the leg you're punching from, in this case the right, then sharp punch up! Bam! Keep your head back; don't lean forward. Keep your eye on your opponent."

Sue imitated his moves, trying over and over.

"Ms. Sue, you're doing fine, but you should be aware of some things to avoid. One, dropping your fists too low—that'll make you vulnerable. Keep your jabs sharp." TiShawn demonstrated. "Two, don't jab into 'space.' Stay close to your body—loop it if you need additional jabs. Whoosh, whoosh!" He looked at Sue to make sure she was paying attention. "Three, don't extend your elbows. Dig under, keep your elbows down, and jab from under. Bam!"

TiShawn had Sue practice for fifteen minutes. It was a satisfying lesson and she started to feel confident about protecting herself.

* * * * *

A little later, Sue hit the Canalway Trail. The late spring days were getting warmer and more and more people were outside enjoying the fresh air. Bicyclists zipped by her from the front and rear; she felt confused which lane to jog on.

Sue was about a half mile down the path, when she ran by a shrub with something dark stuffed inside its dense evergreen branches. She turned around and went back to see what it was. She put her hand in the shrub and partially pulled out a black leather purse with a broken strap. She could see that some items were in it. She got out her cell and called 911.

"911. What is the source of your emergency?"

"I found a purse stuffed into a shrub along the canal. I'm on the trail near South Winton." Sue went on to explain the details.

"A car has been dispatched," the operator told her.

Sue continued to check the trail to see if there was anything else out of the ordinary, no matter how insignificant. There was the typical amount of litter on the path and in the surrounding shrubbery—cigarette butts, disintegrating tissue, an empty energy drink can, beer cans, two pennies, a sales receipt from Walmart, and even a tube of lipstick. She snapped pictures of everything on her phone. Upon closer examination of the sales receipt, she discovered it was from Wednesday and it listed lipstick, paid for in cash. The two items were connected!

Thinking about her last meeting with Lou and the recent canal murder, the missing person's case came to mind. She called Lou on her cell phone.

"Hey. It's Sue. I'm on the canal path and found a purse, a receipt from the Gates Walmart, dated Wednesday at 3:41 p.m., and a new tube of lipstick. This is a long shot, but, by any chance can someone check their surveillance tapes to see if it's our girl?"

"Monica and I will go over there," Lou suggested. "Oh, and good job," he added.

"Don't thank me yet," she admitted before she hung up. "I hope this isn't our girl."

About four minutes later, she saw the familiar Brighton patrol car of Officer Chris Williams. He parked then walked toward her location.

"Hi, Officer Williams," she greeted him with a smile. "The purse is over here," Sue informed him as she went to the shrub and pointed it out. "I touched the strap, not knowing what it was."

He talked into his radio.

Sue continued, "There are also a few items on the ground over here." She walked over to the possible evidence. "Has anyone reported a purse-snatching or a lost purse this morning?" Sue inquired.

"Not yet. You haven't seen anyone in distress, have you?"

"No." They both looked up and down the trail. Outside of cyclists, no one was in sight, except two other officers on their way. As they waited for the other officers to join them, Williams shared some small talk with Sue.

"So, are you getting settled here in Rochester?" he asked.

"I am! I'm training to become a private investigator!" Sue said with pride.

"A private investigator? No kidding!" he said, as the officer's eyebrows raised in surprise. "What made you do that?"

Sue gave Chris the short version of her experience in Delaware. He nodded his head with approval, then added, "Nice. I still have your information, by the way." Chris smiled and winked, and she smiled, too. She felt herself blushing.

The other officers arrived. "Sue, here are Officers Drew Roberts and Sheila McGuire." Sue greeted them.

Officer McGuire took a few photos of the shrub and its contents, put on black laetrile gloves, pulled out the purse, and put it and the other items into evidence bags and sealed them.

Williams asked Sue, "You came from the east, right?"

"Yes."

"Okay, we'll walk to the west for a bit. You may want to stay here."

"If you don't mind, I'm going to take off. You know where to find me if you have any questions," she added.

"Okay, Sue. We'll take it from here. But first, let me walk you back to your car." Officers Roberts and McGuire continued to examine the trail. In some areas of the canal bank, the growth was thick and wild, and important evidence might not be easily discovered.

She hoped her steady, unemotional gaze on Officer Williams wasn't apparent to everyone there, as the gears were turning in her brain. Despite her attraction to him, Sue wanted *"her"* team to get the jump on this case. Not only would solving this missing person's case prove her worth to her new employer, but it may bring a teenage girl back home and keep other women safe. More than ever, Sue knew she had to get moving on this. That meant following her instincts and not waiting for someone to give her instructions. Sue also knew that the more time that goes by, the less chance of finding Emily alive. She hoped she wasn't too late.

18

Officer Christopher Williams took an instant liking to jogger Sue Gainer, an attractive, strong, independent, and smart woman. On the day they met, Chris asked for Sue's ID not only for the required information, but because he wanted to check her out, and have all the information on her, including her phone number. Then Chris could call to update her on the safety of the canal trail, and someday he hoped to know her well enough to perhaps ask her out.

It wasn't that Chris was shy with women; he didn't have any trouble bedding them, but he was shy when it came to Sue. It baffled him. He didn't know how to break the ice with the pretty blonde. Perhaps it was the confident way she approached his cruiser. That day when patrolling, he saw her but had no need to stop and question her—but *Sue* stopped *him*. And then she smiled. His heart responded in a way he didn't expect. It was as if he had never been with a woman before. He had to ask himself, *"Is she the one?"*

Checking out her background was easy. Sue wasn't married. She lived in Delaware for a few years. Sue did not have any traffic violations on her license and her record was clear. No warrants. Her parents, who were responsible citizens, lived in Brighton for almost three decades. There were never any 911 calls placed from that residence.

Today, when he was dispatched to the canal near South Winton, he hoped it would be Sue, but he had no way of knowing. The report was for a purse found on the path—not exactly an emergency—but he put on his lights and sirens to get over there quickly. And he wasn't disappointed. It was Sue. His heart warmed immediately when he saw her—her light hair shining in the sun, her long, firm legs, the tight behind, attractive breasts, and her lovely smile. He felt like a kid again, going on a first date. He "wanted" her, but he knew he had to respect her and take things slowly.

His mind was definitely not on the job at hand. Nevertheless, he had to turn on his body camera and question her just like any other witness.

It appeared that Sue was happy to see him, too, as she gave him a big smile. At least, that was in his favor! This time, he went to her, leaving his cruiser on the side of the road with lights still flashing.

She called him "Officer Williams." He would have to change that soon.

When he saw the purse, he assumed it was a purse snatching. He made a call on his radio, asking about any reported cases. It was negative. That, in itself, was disturbing. Who would not report the theft of their purse? *Perhaps only a dead person,* he worried.

"Miss Gainer?"

"Call me Sue," she offered.

"Sue. Okay." He smiled. "For your safety, you may want to avoid the canal path, at least for now."

"I understand," Sue replied, knowing that someone was out there attacking women.

"Would you like me to let you know when it's safe again?" Avoiding her eyes, his eyes looked off into the distance.

She smiled pleasantly. "Yes. Thank you. That would be great."

Finally, he made eye contact with Sue again and felt a lightness, like a burden had been lifted off of his shoulders. She had given him permission to call on her!

After the other officers joined them, Chris insisted on her immediate safety. "I'll walk you back to your car." He held out his arm, pointing in the direction of the parking lot. If he hadn't been on the job, he might have taken her in his arms and kissed her. It was tempting, but he would have to save that for another time.

He still had a job to do, though—keep his eyes open for any suspicious persons.

However, when Chris went off duty that night, his mind started to wander to thoughts of Sue. He considered asking her out (she wouldn't say no, would she?), giving her a goodnight kiss or two or three (she wouldn't refuse, would she?), and arranging future dates. Perhaps they might even date exclusively, and, naturally, have sex. And what would she be like in bed? He guessed that she might be very demanding. That thought was amusing as he pictured her legs around his body. He couldn't wait for his dreams to come true.

He had several more fantasies before falling asleep. But the one "fantasy" that worried him, that kept interrupting his pleasant dreams, that turned horrific, was that Sue might be the next victim of the Erie Canal killer.

❧ 19 ❧

After Lou was alerted about the sales receipt on the canal path, he and Monica immediately drove to the Gates Walmart and asked to talk to the day manager. Lou showed him his credentials and asked if they could look at the video for Wednesday, particularly at 3:41 p.m. at checkout. He showed Dave, the manager, the photo of the receipt on his phone.

"Ah," Dave said, "That's Operator 004992." He sat down at the computer.

The three of them huddled in the office, while the manager brought up the video a few minutes before the lipstick was purchased. They watched as a young woman walked to the cashier. There was no one in front of her or behind her.

Monica exclaimed, "That's her! That's our missing person!" They watched as she paid for the lipstick in cash and received some change, which she put into her purse.

Lou asked, "Dave, can you start the video when she enters the store?"

Dave backed up the video and they watched the front entrance for about twenty minutes prior to the purchase.

"There! Right there," Monica pointed out. They watched her enter the store and go to Cosmetics. No one was following her.

"Can you see if she went anywhere else in the store?" Lou asked. Dave kept her in view and saw that she also went to Electronics and looked at earbuds for cell phones. She put a pair in her purse.

"Did she just lift those?" Monica remarked incredulously.

"Sure looks like it," Dave said.

As they saw previously, the woman then went directly to the cashier, paid for the lipstick, and put the change in her purse.

"I guess she could afford the lipstick but not the earbuds," Monica said.

Lou suggested, "Let's see if anyone followed her around the store." They looked, but they didn't see any suspicious people following her.

Lou continued, "Okay, let's check the parking lot. Let's see if she gets into a car."

Dave switched to an outside camera. The victim exited the store and walked in a diagonal path to the left of the parking lot. She got into the passenger side of a dark pickup truck. The video was remarkably good, but they couldn't read the license plate. The truck moved to the back of the lot and parked again. It was there for almost 30 minutes, bringing the time to 4:15 p.m.

"So, what were they doing for the last half hour?" Lou wondered out loud.

Monica said with a sly smile, "Well, I can make a guess."

"Sex? Drugs? We may never know," Lou admitted.

"The truck headed in the direction of the 390 expressway," Monica added as she watched the light turn green, allowing a stream of traffic to exit the lot.

"Let's go back to where she enters the store and see if she came out of that same truck."

Dave went back to the earlier time, but this time, expanded the view to the parking lot. There, they saw her arrive in the same truck, exit the passenger door, and walk to the main entrance of the store by herself. The driver of the truck then pulled away and they were able to see him (or her) park in an empty spot, among other parked vehicles, a fair distance from the entrance. Again, the license plate was not readable.

"Let's play the tape back when she leaves in the truck again." Dave replayed it.

Monica pointed out, "Look. There's front-end damage on the driver's side." They tried to get a better look by zooming in on the vehicle. There definitely was a dent in the bumper.

"That'll be a big clue as we look for this guy," Lou said.

Lou stood up. "Thanks for helping, Dave. The police may be asking you for a copy of the video," Lou said as they shook hands. He and Monica left the store.

"We know that our missing person most likely ended up on the canal path because her purse, lipstick, and the receipt were found there. What we don't know is what happened," Lou mulled.

"What's the next step, Lou?"

"I need to find out more about the murder of the first Gates girl. Let's hope our girl didn't meet up with the same perp."

Monica added seriously, "Right. If there's anything more I can do, let me know."

"I will. I'll call Chief Mulroney and see if he has additional information."

As they returned to the office, she announced, "Well, I have a pajama party to go to. Kelsey and I invited Sue."

Lou's thick eyebrows raised up in surprise. "Really? Well now, that will be fun for you."

"Yes, it certainly will." Monica winked and grinned.

Lou shook his head and chuckled as he walked away.

᳇᳇ 20 ᳇᳇

For the entire day on Friday, Sue had been preoccupied with the evidence on the canal path, what Lou might have found out at Walmart and, obviously, Officer Williams. She was attracted to him, yet there was something about him that made her step back. Perhaps it was just his sense of authority or her desire to solve the missing person's case by herself.

But when evening rolled around, she let go of all her distractions and worries and prepared to go to Kelsey's for the pajama party. She really didn't know the girls. But, if she wanted to make new friends in town, what better time than now and with the girls in her new office?

She put on a pair of Joe Boxer pajama bottoms and a large t-shirt. After all, she wanted to be comfortable watching movies, drinking wine, and eating popcorn. She was due at Kelsey's at 9 p.m. On her way, she stopped at Wegmans for a half-gallon of vanilla ice cream for the sundaes. No one even glanced at her pajama bottoms, as it was not unusual behavior to wear them to the store by some standards.

Sue walked up to the door of Kelsey's apartment where she could hear the smooth voice of Usher singing "Nice and Slow," and Monica and Kelsey talking and laughing. *"Sounds like a party!"* Sue thought happily. She knocked on the door.

Monica answered the door, smiling and peeking around the door itself and not showing her body in PJs. "Come in! Welcome to our little party!"

Sue started to walk in, saying, "Thanks for hav..." and then stopped in mid-sentence. Kelsey and Monica were standing there in see-through negligee tops with bikini bottoms—Monica in black and Kelsey in baby blue. Sue fluttered her eyelids because she was so stunned...and obviously overdressed. *"What did I get myself into?"* she panicked. Not to be a "prude," she forced a smile and handed over the ice cream to Kelsey. Monica and Kelsey just laughed because they expected her response.

"Don't worry, Sue. You're among friends. We're just girls being girls," Kelsey said.

"Okayyy," Sue replied with her eyes averted. She didn't want to stare at either one of them but she got an eyeful every time they moved in the room. Kelsey, a fair woman of about 26, was attractive in her blue negligee, with her long, blonde hair falling over her smallish but perky breasts. But Monica, who appeared more exotic at 28, was a knockout in her black negligee—tiny waist, large breasts, long legs. There wasn't anything that Sue couldn't see. Or unsee. And with the Usher song resonating out of the Alexa unit, she thought that she might be in a bordello! She didn't know what to expect next, but she hoped it wasn't "johns!"

No men showed up, much to her relief.

Kelsey showed her to the bedroom where she would sleep. There, Sue dropped off a tote with clothes for the next day.

Not being shy, Sue said with a nervous laugh, "Well, I expected to get to know you, but not quite like this!"

"We didn't want to warn you, because we wanted you to come," Monica spoke in her slight Russian accent. "Don't be afraid. Look, I will brush your hair while you sit and watch TV. Kelsey will dish out some ice cream, and we'll watch James Bond. Won't that be fun?" She went behind Sue's seat on the sofa in the middle of the room and started brushing her hair, but also working her fingers through it with her painted red fingernails. "How does that feel?"

"Good, thanks," Sue replied a little nervously. She noticed that Monica's fingers occasionally touched her face and rubbed her temples. It did feel quite nice. She started to relax.

Kelsey came out from the kitchen with ice cream and a bottle of red wine. "Who wants what?" she asked.

Monica and Sue both said, "Wine!"

"Wine it is!" She returned the ice cream to the freezer and carried three generous glasses of wine into the living room, carefully setting them down on the coffee table.

After a while, Sue was glad that she didn't have to drive home, as the wine was hitting her rather quickly and Kelsey kept refilling her glass.

The three of them watched *From Russia With Love*—of course. Sue started to make comparisons of her new-found friends to the movie's characters Vida and Zora, although they were both dark-haired beauties.

Sue dozed off toward the end of the movie, but woke up about 1 a.m. Neither girl was in the living room, which was now dimly lit by a nightlight, and the television was off. She got up and headed toward the bedrooms. A couple of candles were flickering in Kelsey's room with the door ajar. She glanced in and saw Kelsey and Monica, naked, embracing and kissing. Negligees were crumpled on the floor, as though walked out of. At first, she felt shock, then embarrassment, then curiosity. They didn't seem to notice that she was standing at the door. That is, until Monica caught her eye. "Come in," she invited.

"I, I, I didn't mean to..." Embarrassed, Sue stumbled with her words.

"It's alright, Sue. We're just having a little fun. Would you like to join us?" asked Monica, who got up from the bed totally naked.

"Join you? Um." Sue's mouth was quite dry. She tried to think of something to say. "I think I need some sleep."

Monica walked up to her, her bare skin glowing in the candlelight. "Let me give you a kiss goodnight then." She put her hands gently on both sides of Sue's face and kissed her on the lips. Her breasts snuggled against Sue's body. "You know where to find us, if you need us." She smiled slyly.

"Right," Sue whispered, tasting Monica's lipstick on her lips and noting her heady perfume. "Goodnight, then."

Sue went into her own room but she could hear the moans of passion and lovemaking. It made her horny and wet. She continued to listen until Kelsey and Monica apparently fell asleep. And so did Sue.

* * * * *

Sue awoke Saturday morning, detecting the smell of sausage and eggs cooking. She wandered out of her room in her sleepwear and found a slim, dark-haired man dressed in jeans and a t-shirt at the stove.

He turned, greeting her with a spatula in his hand, "Good morning. You must be Sue. I'm Monica's brother Maxim. You can call me Max. Coffee?"

Sue's mind was foggy and confused. *"When did he show up?"* she wondered. *"And where did he sleep?"* She broke through the fog and replied, "Yes. Coffee. Cream and sugar, if you have it."

"Yes, vanilla creamer okay?"

"Sounds good." She paused, then asked, "Did you sleep here last night or did you just arrive?"

He smiled, knowing what was behind the question. "I came here after the bars closed. I slept on the couch." He handed her a mug of coffee, getting so close she could smell his aftershave lotion. Sue felt a strong and immediate attraction to this man. He exuded sex, much like his sister, and she was intrigued with the hint of Russian accent. It was all very confusing, and Sue was trying to figure out all the emotions in her foggy brain, but it wasn't working.

Sue sat down at the kitchen table, set for four, and sipped from her mug. Max brought over a plate with sliced Polish sausage, eggs, and home fries. It smelled delicious! He smiled with a slightly crooked smile, then went back to the stove to fill another plate.

This was a good chance to look him over. Max had a slightly large nose, dark eyes, long eye lashes, and straight dark hair which never seemed to stay in place. He didn't wear any jewelry.

Kelsey and Monica, already fully dressed, were on their way to the kitchen, giggling again. They sat down at the table and Max delivered their breakfast, then his own, as he joined everyone. They all devoured their meals.

Monica shared the information about Walmart. They all began to speculate.

Kelsey asked, "Why did the girl go from the west side of town to Brighton and the canal path on the east side when the canal was just a few streets away from where she started?"

Max jumped into the conversation, "Perhaps she was with someone she knew and trusted."

Using her "Spidey senses," Sue added, "Maybe she was forced to go. Or maybe she was dropped off and later attacked by a purse snatcher on the canal path."

Monica questioned the young girl's decisions, "Was it planned? Did she plan to meet someone? And did she leave with someone?"

Sue looked at each of her new-found friends sitting around the table, each consuming the breakfast in front of them without consciously enjoying it. "Or is there more to the story?" she added with a note of fear.

They knew they'd have to find out.

"It won't be easy to track the teen because she could have gotten on the canal path anywhere. It's also going to be difficult to track the dark truck across town. We might be able to look for businesses and homes with surveillance cameras near South Winton Avenue," Monica suggested.

Lou hadn't assigned anyone, but they each took a role. Monica planned to look for CCTV cameras along the route. Kelsey would check recent police reports online, and Sue would go back to the canal path.

"Maybe I can find her cell phone on the path," Sue pointed out.

Max interjected, "Sue, I don't think you should go on the canal path by yourself. Let me come with you."

Sue thought about it for a minute. Part of her thought, *"It really might not be safe for a single woman to be alone on the path."* Even Officer Williams would have agreed with that logic. And, she didn't have a permit for her weapon yet. But the other part of her thought, *"If I'm going to be a P.I., then I need to be out there, whether there's danger or not!"*

"Max, thank you, but I can't shirk from danger," Sue told him.

"But we could pose as a couple and have two sets of eyes looking for evidence."

She couldn't deny that. Sue finally agreed to let him come. She went into the bedroom and changed into fresh clothing. He grabbed a light jacket and they both went out to Sue's SUV. After a short drive, she parked in the South Clinton Avenue lot for the canal and walked east toward Winton. They planned to check the path again on the westbound return trip.

As they started their walk, Maxim casually talked to Sue so that it appeared that they were a couple out for a stroll.

"So, Sue, what's your story? Are you in a relationship?" Max pushed away the hair that the breeze had blown across his forehead.

The question startled her since she barely knew Max and she was alone with him on a deserted path. She assumed their conversation would be all about business.

"No. I just moved here from Delaware and am currently living with my parents," she replied, putting up a thin barrier. "What's *your* story?" she asked, throwing the question back to him.

Max grinned. "I'm sure you are wondering about my sister and me. I know she likes to have fun with Kelsey occasionally. I don't mind. It keeps her life interesting—perhaps more exciting for her. I, on the other hand, just like women." He chuckled.

Sue didn't know how to respond to that, so she didn't. Instead, she picked up a stick and started moving the weeds around on the far side of the path, away from the water. Max looked in the dense greenery on the canal side of the path and in the water when there was just a rocky embankment, just in case a body surfaced. The sun was quite warm for early June and some thunderheads were forming in what was a blue sky a few minutes earlier.

Sue's thoughts turned toward any possible evidence they might find. "Max, what do we do with evidence, if we find any?"

"Call 911 if we truly believe that it's evidence and not just trash. We can't touch it or disturb the area around it."

They continued their search, getting closer to Winton Road, which was away from the area where the purse had been found. Sue brushed the weeds back and forth.

"Max! What's this? It looks like earbuds!" With the stick, she pushed back some of the weeds. There, tangled in the tall grass, was a set of white earbuds connected with a white wire. "Is that blood on the wire?" she asked excitedly. Her adrenalin started pumping and her heart rate increased.

Max stared at it for a moment. "It sure looks like blood. Let's take a photo." Sue did, and, once again, she called 911.

"911. What is the source of your emergency?" the dispatcher asked calmly.

"Yes. I found something suspicious on the Canalway Trail. I'm between South Clinton and Winton." Sue gave her name and cell phone number before hanging up.

Max remarked, "Didn't the victim shoplift some earbuds at Walmart?"

"That's what Monica said."

He paused, thinking of all the possibilities. "Now we just wait for the police."

They stood on the paved path and waited about ten minutes for the police to locate them. Officer Williams was one of the responding officers.

Sue smiled when she saw him and he smiled back. "So, we meet again," he said. Then Chris looked at Maxim and wondered who he was. His look was not at all friendly.

After Sue pointed out the earbuds, Officer Williams and two other officers considered the possible evidence. As a result, they called in their Investigative Team who cordoned off the area with crime scene tape, took photos, and put on latex gloves to bag the earbuds.

Sue heard one officer call in the Sheriff's SCUBA Team. A chill went through her body.

Chris remarked, "Sue, I have your information, but I don't have yours." He looked at Max, who pulled out his wallet and handed over his driver's license. Officer Williams jotted down his information, not being able to check him out on his police-issued computer, which was some distance away in his patrol car. He approached Sue privately and asked, "Friend of yours?"

"Well, we just met today. He's the brother of one of my co-workers."

"Hmmm." Thinking of her safety with this stranger, he queried, "You hardly know each other and now you're both out here for a stroll?" Although he was concerned for her safety, there was also a touch of jealousy in his voice, as he, in fact, was feeling quite jealous.

She did not want to reveal their interest in the crime. "We're just being concerned citizens calling in something that didn't look right."

Chris wasn't sure what she was holding back, but there *was* something. He'd find out later. He admonished her, "Well, stay safe. You know you can always call me if you need me."

"Thank you," she said sincerely.

Sue knew the scuba divers would be arriving soon and checking the canal for a body. She and Max would have to leave the area. The thought of a young girl in the canal was disturbing but she'd have to stay tuned for any breaking news.

They began to retrace their steps to Sue's SUV parked in the South Clinton lot, still another 10-minute walk. They started to feel raindrops, lightly at first, and then steadier. There was an overpass ahead, so they went under the bridge to wait out the storm. The rain came down hard and the air turned quite cold, which was not unusual for Rochester. Sue started shivering. Max took off his jacket and gave it to her. Then he put his arm around her shoulders and pulled her to him.

"Body heat," was all he said. Sue, still shivering, was grateful for his warmth. He put his nose into her hair and kissed her head, fondly, as a father would kiss his daughter. She turned to face him somewhat with surprise, wondering why he had kissed her. After all, they had just met. He pulled her to his body and kissed her on the lips. She didn't pull away, but found herself immersed in his gentle kiss, which went on and on. Finally, when their lips parted, Sue opened her eyes and said in a monotone voice, "I'm glad you only like women."

Max laughed heartily.

When the storm ended and the only residual drops were from the leaves on the trees, Sue and Max ventured away from the bridge and into the returning sunlight. They stepped up their pace to the car, anxious to tell the others what they had discovered and about the scuba team. But not about the kiss.

❧ 21 ❧

Even though it was a weekend, Lou Perlo and the four members of his agency team sat at the conference room table discussing the breaking news.

Lou reported to his team, "A body was found in the canal, caught on some rock netting. Having been in the water for a few days, the body was in the state of decomposition and no facial recognition could be made. Monroe County's Medical Examiner's Office took custody of the body but is not making any statements about the identity of the victim until the family is notified and they know the cause of death."

But based upon their leads, Lou's team was quite sure who the victim was—Emily Rogers. His team also talked about the earbuds, the surveillance video in the Walmart parking lot, and the dark-colored truck.

Lou spoke up. "We assume that the truck headed for the expressway. Unfortunately, we don't have the tag number or we could have traced it by the license plate readers along the way. But Monica found several businesses with surveillance cameras and we have the approximate time. If we see that the same truck got on the expressway near Walmart and off the expressway near the canal on the east side, then there's a good chance that it belongs to the killer."

Everyone agreed. He continued, "Monica and Max, check out each one of those cameras. Kelsey, I need you to see if Emily had a bank account and if there were any transactions. Also, ask the police if have her cell records yet. Search the web for *anything* related to our missing person. Sue, you and I are going back to see Emily's mother. We also need to find out if there's a connection to the other Gates teen."

They all stood and left for their assignments.

* * * * *

Emily's mother looked tearful as she led Lou and Sue into her living room.

"I've been crying since the police told me about the body in the canal," she told them. "If it's my baby girl," she wept into her handful of tissues, "I never got to say, 'I love you!'" She continued to sob. "Why would anyone want to kill her?"

"I'm so sorry, Mrs. Rogers," Lou remarked with sincerity. "I know the police were already here and asked you some questions, but since you hired me to look into Emily's disappearance, would it be okay if we asked you a few more questions now?"

She nodded without looking up.

"Okay. Do you remember anything more of where Emily went that day?"

"No. She turned off her phone early on, so I couldn't track her. That's the first thing I tried to do. Then I didn't check again."

"Did the police find her phone?"

"No. She *always* had her phone. She did everything on that phone. The killer probably stole it."

"Do you know if Emily was friends with Sarah Bennington?"

At first, Mrs. Rogers was puzzled, although the name was familiar. "Oh, the girl who was found in the canal a few weeks ago? No, I don't remember ever hearing Emily mention that name."

Sue spoke up. "Would you mind if we looked at Emily's bedroom?"

"Sure," Mrs. Rogers agreed as she stood and led them down a short hallway.

There was barely room for the dresser or full-sized bed, but it was clearly a teenager's bedroom, with an unmade bed, posters on the walls, and jewelry, makeup, and several bottles of colorful nail polish on the small maple dresser.

Sue took out a pen from her purse and turned over a few other things on the dresser—receipts, seventy-five dollars in cash, and a box of tampons.

"Well, I don't think she was pregnant," Sue mumbled to Lou. "I wonder where she got the seventy-five dollars." Looking closely at a hand-written receipt, she read aloud, "'One wooden box.' Dated last week. That's odd. Mrs. Rogers, do you know anything about a wooden box?"

"Hmm. Can't say I do."

"How about a man named Dan Gilson?"

"No." She shook her head, somewhat confused.

Sue looked at Lou. "Could be our suspect."

Mrs. Rogers picked up one of Emily's t-shirts and cried into it. "What am I going to do without her?" She went to put the t-shirt back when she noticed the tear. "Oh, I wonder what happened here?"

Lou looked at the shirt as Mrs. Rogers handled it, but it didn't look particularly suspicious. "I'd like you to keep her room like it is for a while in case we, or the police, need to check it again." She nodded her response.

They thanked Mrs. Rogers and promised that they'd get to the bottom of this and find justice for her daughter.

As Lou and Sue returned to the car, they sat silently for a few minutes, staring out the window and thinking about their next steps.

"That Dan Gilson might be the boyfriend or the killer or both," Sue finally said.

Lou responded, "See if you can find a phone number and address for him."

Sue researched Dan on her phone. "Got him. He doesn't live far from here." She gave him the address on Transit Road and they headed to his residence.

When they arrived at his house, fifty-five-year-old Dan Gilson had his garage door open as he stood over a table saw, which was slicing through a piece of lumber and spewing sawdust into the air. He brushed off the shavings and examined the finished product in his hand. It was perfect and he was pleased.

Dan stopped and looked out from the garage when he saw the unfamiliar car pull in. He was quite distrustful of strangers and wondered why these two were in his driveway. Dan stood a little straighter in his overalls, feeling pain in the small of his back. He had been bending over the saw too long. As two occupants got out of the car—a man and a woman— he removed his goggles and brushed off the remainder of the sawdust from his clothing. He picked up a screwdriver for protection, just in case, and put it in the pocket of his overalls.

"You want something?" Dan asked gruffly, his demeanor unfriendly.

Lou reached out to shake his hand but Dan didn't reciprocate. "My name is Lou Perlo, Private Investigator, and this is Sue Gainer." He showed him his license. "Mind if we ask you a few questions?"

Dan looked at the license. "Detective Agency?" with the emphasis on "detective."

"We're *private* investigators working on a case, and we're hoping you can help."

"What do you need from me?" he questioned, stroking the gray stubble on his chin.

"Do you know a teenager named Emily Rogers?" Lou inquired.

"Emily...Emily." Dan took a few moments to consider whether or not to lie. Then he showed a moment of enlightenment. "Oh! Emily! That cute little girl with that funny blue hair! She looked like, whaddya call it? A smurf! Yeah, that's it! A smurf!" Dan had a wide grin when he talked about her.

"How exactly do you know her, Mr. Gilson?"

Dan's lip started twitching. He didn't want to give himself away.

"Bought a finely made wooden box from her. Yes, sirree. Look. I have it right on my shelf." He walked to a cluttered shelf in the garage and retrieved what appeared to be an expensive, hand-sculpted piece of art in two different woods—maple and cherry. "Paid her seventy-five dollars for it! A real bargain, I think! Found it on Craigslist."

"Did she say where she got it?" Sue questioned.

"No, uh, but it looks like it came from one of those art-and-craft shows at the museum." Then his expression changed to one of concern. "She didn't steal it, did she?"

"Hmm, interesting concept. If she stole the earbuds, what's to say she didn't steal the box?" Lou thought to himself. He responded, "Not that we know of. Was there anything in the box when she sold it to you?"

"Huh! I actually can't say. I haven't figured out how to open it! I think there must be a special way, y'know, like a secret compartment."

Sue asked, "Mr. Gilson, would it be okay if we borrowed this from you for a few weeks while we work on this case?"

He was silent, not willing to work with them nor get himself involved. Then he had second thoughts. What if the police showed up and gave him trouble? That was the deciding factor.

He surrendered the box. "I want it back," he insisted in no uncertain terms.

Lou handed Dan his business card. "Thank you. Here's my number. Call if you remember anything else about Emily and the box."

In a deceptive voice, he said, "Sure thing, Mr. Perlo. I hope she's okay. She sure is a pretty little lady with a nice smile."

Lou looked into Dan's eyes and said, "I'm sorry to say she's missing."

"Missing?!" He seemed startled by this news. To Lou, he seemed sincere in his concern.

"We have reason to believe she may have been a victim of foul play."

"Who the hell would hurt her?"

"That's what we're going to find out."

As they left, Dan thought smugly, *"That little bitch deserved everything that she got!"*

22

When it comes to murder, the investigation doesn't stop for the weekend. Nor do the detectives get to go home and sleep when they're tired. They work the case until the leads dry up or the suspects are locked up and the case is solved.

Detectives Steve Grant of Monroe County's Criminal Investigations' Major Crime Unit and Brian Sills of the Brighton Police's Investigative Unit partnered up to question persons of interest in the cases of Emily Rogers and Sarah Bennington, now both confirmed as homicides. Detective Grant also worked with the New York State Police who were initially involved, and the Gates PD who needed to solve the murders of two of their residents on the Erie Canal.

As an exhausted Grant returned to his desk on Sunday morning, Sills informed him, "You got two on ice."

Dan Gilson and Tristen Phillips were picked up and brought to Major Crimes for interrogation. After reviewing their records and observing each on the camera monitor, they decided to tackle Tristen first. They believed he would be the easiest to crack since he was young and nervous.

The twenty-one-year-old was notably nervous, biting his nails, holding his head, and rubbing his tired eyes. He stood up, walked around the room, and sat back down. He couldn't sit still for a second. Detective Grant wondered if he was on "something," like meth. He knew that meth addicts have exaggerated mannerisms and a need to keep themselves busy at all times. Their dilated eyes dart around, often experiencing paranoia. He'd check him closely once he entered the room.

Grant picked up a pad and pen and went into Interview Room #1, and Sills followed. Tristen anxiously looked up.

"Hi, Tristen. I'm Detective Steve Grant. This is Detective Brian Sills. I assume you know why you're here." He pushed a can of soda pop across the table to Tristen.

"About Emily," Tristen replied then burst into tears, wiping his nose on his shirt when he was done crying.

"Yes, Emily. What is your connection to her?" Sills asked.

"She's my girlfriend! I love her!" Then he shed a few more tears then had another sip of pop.

"I'm sorry for your loss. How did you meet Emily?"

He closed his eyes as he recalled the moment he fell in love. "I met her on a haunted hayride last October. We were both hired to scare people. She was a witch. Her hair was dyed black and her face was purple and she had red lips. And I was a mad magician with an evil face, setting off smoke bombs and having a scary guy jump out of a large box." Tristen opened his eyes, wide. "Everyone screamed.

Haha!" Then Tristen looked sad again. "We'll never do that together anymore."

Grant interrupted. "It says here that you *are* a magician."

Tristen smiled for the first time. "Yes, I am! Emily loved my card tricks! I'm a car mechanic, too. I work with my dad."

"Good, good. Did you know Sarah Bennington, too?"

He quizzically looked at the detective. "Who?"

Grant jotted down a note on his pad.

Sills spoke up. "Let's move on. Let's talk about June 6th. What did you do that day?"

A sigh escaped Tristen's lungs. "I drove to Emily's house to apologize, but she turned her back on me!"

"What were you apologizing for?"

He hesitated, looked away, and wrung his hands, which Grant noticed and recognized as a sign of guilt. "Um. Well, I told her that she needed to stop shoplifting. She got upset and tried to get out of my truck. I was begging her to stay and...and I tried to stop her." He left out the part about ripping her shirt. He took another sip from the pop can.

In a calm, quiet voice, Grant asked, "Did you, in any way, injure her?" He looked directly into Tristen's eyes, which appeared to have pupils of a normal, sober person.

"No. No, sir." He shook his head. There was a moment of silence in the room as they tried to determine whether or not he was lying.

"Okay, so you apologized, and she left in anger?"

"Yes, but after a few minutes, I decided to follow her."

The detective's eyebrows raised. "Oh? And where did she go?"

"To Elmgrove Gas. You know, the one with the crazy LED lights. An old guy in a truck picked her up."

The detective nodded. "So what did you do?"

"I was mad and wondered what she was doing hanging out with such an old fart."

"Can you give us a description of this guy?" Sills asked.

"I could only see his head and his arms in the truck. He was maybe 60. Graying hair. A little heavy."

"A good description of Dan Gilson in the next room," Grant thought.

"Was that the last time you saw Emily?"

"Well, no. I followed them to a run-down house on Transit Road. I think the old guy must live there." Grant wrote that on his pad. Tristen continued, "Next thing I knew, Emily was running down the driveway. I saw her run to the Burger Barn and go inside."

"Did you go inside the Burger Barn?"

"No. I waited in the parking lot to see if the old guy followed her."

"And did he?"

He thought about it for a moment. "Not sure. Twenty minutes later, somebody else in a truck picked up Emily. No one I knew."

Both Grant and Sills wrote down this information. The detectives listened to the rest of his statement then excused themselves. Leaving Tristen alone with his can of soda pop, they went to see Dan Gilson in the next room.

Dan was resting comfortably on the cushioned, metal chair with his arms crossed against his belly. It was a sign that he really didn't want to reveal anything, especially to the police. He had been interrogated several times in his life and he knew what to say, what not to say, and when to ask for his attorney.

He wasn't outwardly nervous, but Dan frequently rubbed the gray stubble on his chin.

"Hi, Dan. My name is Detective Steve Grant with Major Crimes. And this is Detective Brian Sills." They sat across from Mr. Gilson.

"From our records, we see that you've been 'out' for a few years now and you've been staying out of trouble."

Dan grunted and his lip twitched a bit. He looked away rather than at the detective's face.

"You're here today about Emily Rogers. Exactly, how do you know her?"

Interrogation was not new to Dan. He was familiar with the game. He carefully explained about seeing the ad on Craigslist and buying the carved wooden box from her, simplifying the details. He told them only what they needed to know.

Watching Gilson carefully, Sills asked, "Did you also know Sarah Bennington?"

"Name doesn't ring a bell."

Grant showed Dan a photo from Sarah's social media page, since the pictures of the bloated body from the morgue did not resemble Sarah in life. Dan pushed the photo back and he shook his head.

"Never saw her before in my life."

If he and Tristen were telling the truth, perhaps there was no connection between the two murders. Grant decided to change the subject.

"Okay, Dan. When was the last time you saw Emily?"

"June 6th."

"Tell us about that day."

"Well, I couldn't open the wooden box. It was a puzzle, you see. I thought she could open it being a teenager and all. So I asked her to stop by and show me how."

"And did she?"

"Did she 'stop by'?" Dan repeated. "Yes."

"How did she get to your house?"

"I agreed to pick her up at a gas station on Elmgrove and give her a ride." Grant knew this agreed with Tristen's statement.

"Did she open the box?"

"She tried, but she left without opening it."

"Why is that?"

Dan shrugged his shoulders.

"We have a witness saying she ran out of your driveway that afternoon," Sills interjected.

Dan's eyes opened wide and stared at the detective. *What witness?* he wondered. Dan didn't have time to think carefully about his answer.

"Guess she had to catch a bus," he said without blinking.

"Why didn't you drive her back to the gas station?" Grant asked.

Dan lied, "She had some other places to go."

"I don't think you're telling us the truth, Dan. Why would she run out of your house minutes after getting there?" Grant paused then asked seriously, "Did you follow her, Dan? Did you hurt her? Did you strangle and kill Emily Rogers?"

Thoughts raced through his mind about Emily kicking him in the groin and how he doubled over in pain. He also remembered wanting to teach her a lesson.

Puckering his lips, he simply said, "No."

Detective Grant looked him in the eye. He was convinced that Dan was lying. If he learned of any evidence to prove that Gilson was lying, he'd see him put back behind bars. But, for now, he didn't have any reason to hold him. There was more investigating to be done.

"Alright, Gilson. You can go." Then as a second thought, Grant added, "And don't leave town!"

If he needed Dan to take a lie detector test, he'd have his men pick him up again. For now, he'd check with the crime lab on the status of their earbud test results and call the Perlo Agency to see if they had any leads.

There was still one nagging question: who was the man who picked up Emily at the Burger Barn? Where did they go and what happened after that?

Grant and Sills also needed to prove that Tristen and Dan did not follow Emily and the unknown male. For that, they'd need someone to check surveillance cameras.

After Dan and Tristen left, Steve went back to Room #1 and collected the pop can, which Tristen drank from, for DNA. He immediately sent it to Rochester's newly built Crime Lab, which had all the latest technology as well as expertise.

Back at his desk, Steve Grant called to one of his super-sleuth assistants, forty-year-old Mary Collins, who was walking by. "Hey, Mary! Any word on those phone records from Emily Rogers and Sarah Bennington?"

"I'll check." She disappeared for a few minutes then reappeared at Steve's desk. "They just came in."

Together they went through the list of numbers Emily called as well as her text messages from that day. Emily texted several people including Dan and someone named Rich. There was one number that stood out; a number that Emily had called just before her disappearance. And it matched the number from the text to Rich. Mary got on her computer and did a search—it was a burner phone.

They also checked the number against Sarah's calls and texts, but there was no match.

Steve slyly grinned as he said to Mary, "Why don't we give this Rich guy a call?" Mary smiled as well and nodded.

But Steve got a recording that said, "The number you have called is not in service. Please try again," followed by a long, monotonous tone.

"Damn!" Steve said as he slammed the phone down. "Well, there's one thing we know for certain. He's on to us."

23

Lou continued to work through Sunday. He called the parents of Sarah Bennington and asked if he might have a conversation with them about their daughter's murder. They agreed to talk.

He pulled into the driveway of a rather expensive one-story gray-brick house with a stone façade. The back of the house looked out over a private golf course. Lou realized that Sarah came from a family with a much different financial status than Emily's.

A well-dressed woman in her late forties answered the door. She had the look of money.

"Every day I wake up and think it must be a bad dream," Sarah's mother lamented as they sat on the sofa in the formal living room. "Then I remember that it's real. She was Daddy's girl. My husband took it especially hard."

Mr. Bennington, who was sitting in a leather recliner, agreed by shaking his head while fighting back his tears. He was speechless.

Mrs. Bennington continued, "Have you found out who did this?"

"No, not yet," Lou admitted. "I've been asked to investigate the Emily Rogers missing person's case and I need to know if there was any connection between the two girls."

"Hmm. I heard that they just pulled another body out of the canal. Was it your missing person?"

"They did find a body, and it was a homicide, but there's been no public positive identification yet."

"Terrible. I can't imagine what her parents are going through."

Lou asked, "Do you know if Sarah knew Emily?"

"I don't think so." She went on to tell Lou about her schooling and college plans.

"Do you know if they were friends on social media?"

"Well, her page is still up. Let's take a look." Mrs. Bennington led him to their desktop computer in the expansive family room with hardwood floors, an oriental carpet, facing loveseats, and a large fireplace. She hit a few keys and Sarah's page came up. Lou examined her profile photo. Sarah was a lovely, tall, slim girl with a style all her own. She wore large sunglasses, a bikini top, and a pair of shorts. Wisps of her golden hair, straight and somewhat thin, blew in the breeze. Her smile showed perfect white teeth.

Mrs. Bennington scrolled down. "Okay, here are her friends." Emily was not among them.

"Can we look at her male friends?"

She complied, slowly scrolling as Lou took a careful look at each one of them. He didn't recognize anyone nor were there any familiar names. Several were from France.

They also looked at her recent messages on the site. Lou wrote down the four or five names of the people who sent her notes on the day of her murder.

"Do you know if she had a boyfriend or was on any dating sites?"

"Sarah? I don't think she would date anyone she didn't know."

"May I take a look around her bedroom?"

"Yes. It's just the way she left it," her mother explained. They went down a small hallway to the end room.

The room was not typical for a teenager, but rather elegant and well kept. The bed was made, posters of Paris were on her walls, and a small replica of the Eiffel Tower sat on her desk.

"Looks like she was into France."

"Yes, she was an exchange student in Paris for a year. She spoke fluent French."

Lou casually looked on Sarah's dresser and desk. There was nothing out of place, no notes, nothing that stood out as unusual.

"She had her whole life ahead of her," sobbed Mrs. Bennington. "She was brilliant! Now she's gone. Never to fulfill her dreams. Never to get married or have children." She burst into tears, dabbing a tissue under her carefully applied eye makeup. Her husband came to her and put his arms around her. She turned to cry on his shoulder.

"It's okay, Liz," he comforted. "I'm here."

"Thank you, Mr. and Mrs. Bennington," Lou sincerely said, feeling their grief. "I'm so sorry for your loss. I appreciate the time you gave me. If you think of anything else, here's my card." He handed it to Mr. Bennington and then went to the door and let himself out.

It seemed like he was holding his breath all the while he was inside, so he let out a big breath, trying to let go of the heaviness he felt.

"Two girls. Two families torn by grief. I need to get to the bottom of this," he softly said out loud to himself as he got behind the wheel of his car. "I need to help these families. It's the least I can do."

⚮ 24 ⚮

Back in the office on Monday morning, Lou asked Sue to come into his office. "I have a new job for you."

She nodded and followed him inside.

Lou closed his door and they both sat down. First of all, tomorrow we need to speak to this Tristen Phillips and see what he has to say."

"Agreed," Sue said.

"Now, here's an insurance fraud case that I need you to handle," Lou explained. He showed her a picture of an aging black man on crutches, taken with a telephoto lens.

"This is Marvin LaDue. The insurance company hired us to look into the validity of his injuries after being hit by a car on South Avenue. The driver of the car stayed on scene and gave a report to the police. The insurance company has reason to believe that Mr. LaDue is faking his injuries."

"Why is that?"

"Apparently, he had a similar claim in March just a block away from the most recent accident. In both cases, he was clipped by cars, refused treatment by EMTs, then filed claims with the insurance company using the police report." Lou gave her a copy of the most recent report with the name and address of the driver and a witness. "The insurance company paid him for the first claim."

"Were there any surveillance videos of the latest accident?"

"That's your job to find out. We also need you to surveil Mr. LaDue to see if he slips up and walks without his crutches. Ask Kelsey or Monica to get you the equipment you need from the storage room."

Excited about her new solo assignment, Sue immediately went to see Kelsey.

As Sue looked around the storage room with Kelsey, she had an idea. Along with her equipment for the new case, she also borrowed a GPS unit, magnetized to attach to a suspect's vehicle. Kelsey set it up and explained how to track it on her phone. *"Hmm, this is going to come in handy,"* Sue thought.

* * * * *

Sue left for her surveillance job with a digital camera and telephoto lens, a button camera, and a pair of binoculars. She drove to the scene of the accident and parked.

The city's "red-light" cameras had recently been removed, so that didn't help. Her first stop was at a small diner on the corner of South Avenue where the accident allegedly occurred. No outside cameras. None at a hair salon across the road either. Sue lucked out at a bar, which had cameras covering its own parking lot, but it was difficult to ascertain whether the accident was staged (or not) from the camera angle as well as the distance to the street. Sue was feeling a bit discouraged. She decided to go to the alleged victim's residence and set up her surveillance there.

Things were uneventful until 4 p.m. when seventy-five-year-old Marvin LaDue opened his door to get his mail. He was a thin black man with gray hair and a grizzled beard. Sue snapped a digital image of him reaching into the small postal box, which was screwed into the siding, and pulling out a few white envelopes. It really didn't prove much. She continued to watch.

Twenty minutes later, the door opened again. This time Marvin exited using a pair of crutches. Being careful of his left leg, he maneuvered down the four porch steps to the sidewalk and hobbled to the corner where there was a liquor store. He went inside. Sue moved her car and also went inside the store, engaging the hidden camera in a buttonhole on her shirt.

Marvin was in a friendly conversation with the clerk. "Yessirree, remember that time when Charles Murray, 'The Natural,' won the junior welterweight title in '93? I was there!"

"You was there? Nah. I don't believe it," the store owner rebuffed.

"I swear on my mother's grave! In 'lantic City! That was some night! I'll never forget it!"

"You sure got a lot of stories, Marvin."

"They's all true, too." He paused. "Well, how about two of those ten-dollar scratch-offs and some of that Jim Beam?" Marvin pointed to the items behind the counter.

"Let's see your cash first."

"Yeah, yeah," he complained. Marvin rested his crutches against the counter as he dug into his pocket and pulled out a wad of bills held together with a large paper clip.

The store clerk noted all his cash. "Hey, Marvin, when did you become so rich?"

"Shhh, now. We don't want to let the world know, now do we?" He looked over his shoulder and noticed Sue in the New York Wines aisle. They had a clear view of each other, but Marvin didn't suspect she would roll him as he walked home. He turned back to the store clerk, pulled out three twenties and waited for change. Once in his hand, he stuffed the money and instant lottery tickets into his pocket and took the paper bag with the bottle of bourbon.

"Thanks, man. Gonna have a good time tonight!"

"Are you celebratin' something?"

"Oh, I drink to my health," he laughed as he stepped away from the counter holding up his purchase. He took two steps on each foot before realizing he didn't have his crutches.

"Oops. Forgot my crutches! Heh heh."

Sue snapped two or three shots on her small spy camera. She didn't approach Marvin but allowed him to leave the liquor store.

He was now more observant of his surroundings and made sure he hobbled on his crutches. But it was certainly more difficult for him to hold a large, heavy bottle in a paper bag while using two crutches. It swung back and forth but Marvin was careful not to rip the paper bag and lose its precious cargo.

He disappeared beyond the store's window and Sue immediately followed him out. Shockingly, he was nowhere in sight! She knew he turned right, so where did he go? She headed in that direction, stepping up her gait.

Suddenly she found herself tripping over an unknown object in her path and falling to the ground, scraping her hands and knees on the sidewalk and nearly hitting her chin. Before she could get up, she felt something forcefully poking her in the small of her back.

"Aha!" said Marvin, pushing his crutch into her back. "I had a feelin' you was followin' me. Trying to rob me, huh?" He clunked her on the head with the crutch, then returned it to her back.

"Ow! Hey, stop it!" Sue, feeling helpless, pleaded with her attacker. "I was just going to my car," she lied. She tried to remember if her training included being caught by the suspect.

"Uh huh. Well, get outta here before I call the police." He removed his crutch from her back and allowed her to get up. "Stupid bitch," he mumbled.

She got herself to her feet, brushed off her hands and knees, then looked at Marvin. He was leaning on both crutches and displaying a scowl on his whiskered face.

"Go on! Get!" He pointed the way with one crutch. She left.

Sue hoped that the pictures she took might be enough evidence, so she went back to the office and told Lou what happened. As he downloaded the photos, he looked at Sue in her disheveled state and started chuckling. "So, he caught you following him."

"Yeah. I wasn't as careful as I should have been."

"Well," he started, hesitantly. "It just shows you that you have to be very cunning out there and outsmart the other guy. Expect the unexpected. Be prepared for anything! You can thank your lucky stars that he isn't a dangerous felon and wasn't carrying a gun." Lou paused as he gave her a moment to consider her mistakes. "I'll see what the insurance company says about the pictures. If it's enough, then our job is done. If not, you'll be watching Mr. LaDue again."

Sue sat back in the guest chair and groaned. She had a feeling she would be on another stakeout with Marvin, but now he might recognize her, so she'd have to be more covert.

❧ 25 ❧

Kelsey knocked on Lou's office door and walked in. Lou was going over the Emily Rogers case with Sue, Monica, and Max.

Monica was saying, "We checked out ten cameras. Two weren't operational. But we did review the other eight tapes."

Max jumped in, "We saw the same black truck all the way from the Gates Walmart to the canal on Clinton. Couldn't make out the driver or the license plate, though. It looked like a male and a passenger."

Lou was hoping for a real break. "Were you able to follow the truck after it left the canal parking lot?"

The office door opened, and Kelsey burst in.

"Sorry to interrupt," Kelsey said as she read off a scribbled phone memo sheet. "I've got Emily's cell phone records courtesy of the RPD! The last ping was in the area of Winton Road by the canal. During the previous seven days, she called two numbers several times and received calls back, and there was another number who called her twice. I looked up the numbers. The first number belongs to a Tristen Phillips, the second number came from a burner phone. And the person who called her twice is a guy named Dan Gilson. Tristen and Dan were both interviewed by the RPD today. There were also texts to a guy named Rich."

"Dan Gilson! Thanks, Kelsey." Lou then said to Sue, "Well, it seems that good ol' Dan must have a very poor memory. He had a hard time remembering Emily except for her hair. But we know now that he's keeping something from us."

Monica wanted to answer Lou's earlier question before Kelsey walked in. "Lou, we saw the black truck get back on the expressway, but we don't know where he got off."

"Okay. I think we need to follow up with Dan Gilson again. I wonder if the RPD had any success with him." He dialed the direct number of Detective Grant.

"Hey, Steve. Lou Perlo here. I understand you interviewed Dan Gilson today."

"We didn't get much out of him. Pretty tight-lipped. Not sure he's telling the truth. How about you?"

"I've got Sue Gainer working the case and she's got an idea or two. We're trying to trace that throw-away phone to a credit card, but that may take time."

Steve admitted, "We don't have anything to hold either one of them right now. Neither seems to know Sarah Bennington. If we hear anything, we'll share it with you."

"Great. Same here. Bye."

After a moment, Lou turned to Sue. "What do you think we should do?" giving her a chance to make a deduction based on what they had learned today.

Sue stared into the distance with the gears turning in her head. "I think it's all about the box. I need to see what's inside!"

❧ 26 ❧

Sue was facing a dilemma—she had too many pokers in the fire and she was feeling inadequate and overwhelmed.

The next morning, just before dawn, she drove to Ontario Beach Park in the Charlotte neighborhood and headed for the pier where the Genesee River meets Lake Ontario. She hadn't been there in many years. Sue walked to the lighthouse at the end of the pier to watch the sunrise. It was glorious! The warm sun rose quickly, giving birth to a new day. She watched the squawking seagulls flying high in the sky and she looked out upon the vast swath of sandy beach. A couple of boats were slowly advancing in the channel, ready to go out onto the open waters of the great lake. Nearby, Sue spotted the carousel building. It was too early in the day for it to be operational, but she had many fond memories riding the various, expertly carved, painted, wooden animals there, with her hands on the thick pole and her feet in leather stirrups, and the cranking rods that made the animals go up and down. In her mind's eye, she could hear the calliope playing, the children laughing, and see the curious painted pictures from another age. She sighed.

As the sun continued to energize her, Sue's mind turned to her responsibilities.

First and foremost was her dad's illness. That was the main reason for moving back to Rochester. She had promised to be there when her parents needed her and to provide emotional and physical support. She couldn't let them down. That meant taking her dad to treatments and helping her mom with the household chores and yardwork. Now that she had a job, it was impossible to be everywhere at once. She needed to make sure this remained her top priority.

Next was Sue's commitment and performance working for Lou, requiring her to be available 24/7. That meant Sue needed to dedicate most of her time away from home to ongoing training and Lou's paying clients. Not only was it an assignment, but her own main objective was to find the killer of one, or perhaps two teenage girls, whose bodies were found in the canal. Plus, she still had the insurance fraud case to prove.

Sue also agreed to help her friend Carrie, whose ex, Jared, was giving her a hard time. That situation could possibly escalate to domestic violence if preventative measures were not in place. Sue felt she was still lacking the necessary information about Jared and needed to step up her involvement. She would not rest until she felt that Carrie and her family were safe.

Most recently was her relationship with Maxim. It was a new wrinkle that she had not anticipated. She found herself daydreaming and wanting physical contact with Max. Sue knew that she really needed to focus on her responsibilities and Max needed to do the same. Could they keep the two separate but enjoy each other at the same time? Was it ethical for them to date a co-worker? She tried to convince herself that it was acceptable because he was just on contract with Lou. He could leave and take on a job somewhere else if he wanted. And what about Officer Williams? The jury was still out on that relationship, if there was one.

Walkers and fishermen started populating the pier, so Sue went back to her SUV to begin her workday.

She looked up Jared's address on her phone. In twenty minutes, she was in front of a sleepy brick bungalow with a white SUV in the driveway.

"That's odd," Sue whispered to herself. "Where's the truck?" She stared at the vehicle for a few moments, puzzled.

Then it dawned on her that Jared was trying to get a car loan. Maybe this was his new vehicle. She wondered who the sucker was who co-signed the loan.

A privacy fence prevented her from seeing his backyard but there was an empty lot next door. Sue parked in front of the vacant lot, exited her vehicle, and walked towards Jared's driveway. The detective-in-training checked to make sure there was no one either in the SUV or outside the house. There were no open curtains nor was anyone peeking out. She nonchalantly walked up to the SUV. There was a "new car sticker" on the passenger-side back window. At the cargo area of the SUV, she bent over and stuck a magnetized GPS unit in a secure spot. Sue quickly went back to her own vehicle, opened the app, and saw a large, red arrow pointing to the location of the SUV. It worked.

It was also her plan to come back and have another look around. And she'd know if he went anywhere near Carrie and their child or Carrie's mother. Judy was someone Sue hadn't considered before! She could be in as much danger as Carrie, especially when she was babysitting. She made a mental note to put her phone number in her contact app.

Sue looked at her fitness watch. It was time to attend a self-defense class, an ongoing class for eight weeks but she could choose to take it early in the day or later at night. She appreciated the flexibility of the instructor, Ross Rizzo, a retired New York state trooper. The write-up on Rizzo mentioned that many injuries and crimes were preventable if victims knew how to defend themselves. Sue was ready to learn how to do that.

* * * * *

Ross began the one-student session, "Sue, there are a few basic moves for you to learn today. You'll go through the motions with me and then I'll let you take control."

Sue was a bit nervous. Ross was a big guy. "Okay," she said nervously.

"Here are three basic moves: aim for the throat with your forearm. Use your entire body." He showed her in slow motion, stepping forward with one leg then using his weight to execute the move. "Now you try it on me." Sue did.

Ross explained, "Did you see my reaction? It made me move my head back and my body out. This is when you take your elbow, again using your body weight, and jab it right into my solar plexus—the soft spot under my ribcage." Sue made the motion.

"Okay, now that I'm doubled over from your jab to my solar plexus, take this opportunity to knee my groin. Once again, you are going to have to step forward, then knee. Good. Let's do all three again."

"Throat, solar plexus, groin," Sue repeated the move three times.

"Great. Now here are some additional defense moves. Let's say a guy grabs your arm." He demonstrated. "Twist your hand to get out of his grip." That seemed fairly easy for Sue to do.

"Now, here's what you need to do to disable him. Grab his wrist with your opposite hand. Point your elbow up, and make a 'slice' down, using your body strength. Bam! He loses his grip and you're in control."

Sue was getting the feel of it now. She smiled at Ross in gratitude.

He continued. "What if a guy comes from behind and puts his hands on your throat? Your first instinct is to grab his hands, right?" Sue nodded. "Instead of clawing, grab the attacker's arms and pull yourself towards him. Swing your hips to one side. Make a fist and hit his groin!"

She tried it a few times. It wasn't second nature to her, but in time, she wouldn't have to think about it and just do it.

Ross had her go through all the moves again, step by step. "Okay, Sue. Next time we'll make sure you remembered what you learned today, plus you'll have more defense moves to learn. Good job today."

* * * * *

Sue freshened up at home, spent some time with her dad, and then put the strange box on the kitchen table and tried to open it. There was nothing visible or apparent—no seams or indents or unusual markings. She used her index finger and pushed here and there, especially where there was a change in wood inlay. She turned it upside down and every whichway. Shook it, rolled it, squeezed it. Nothing. She thought, *"Maybe it opens by a timer. Or a remote. Then what would I do?"*

Her dad came to the table. "What is *that?*"

"Supposedly it's a box, but I can't figure out how to open it."

"It looks like a puzzle. Let me take a look." He slid his finger down on the cherry inlay, turned the top to unlock it, and it opened effortlessly. Sue couldn't believe her eyes.

"How the heck did you do that?"

"Haha. Takes an engineer in computer science, I guess."

"Thanks, Dad. What would I do without you?" After Sue spoke those words, they both looked at each other, understanding the sadness behind the words that they both felt.

"Don't worry, sweetie. I'll beat this cancer."

"I know you will, Dad." She hoped he was right.

When Mr. Gainer went into the living room to watch television, Sue focused again on the box.

Inside the small drawer of the wooden box was a red-and-black thumb drive, held in place with rubber cement. She put on a pair of vinyl gloves that she had in a first-aid kit, pulled out the thumb drive, and thought. *"I need to check this out right now."* Sue stood up and headed for her bedroom.

Upstairs, at her computer, Sue inserted the thumb drive. A folder popped up that said "Trolley." She clicked on it. There were several image icons, so Sue started opening them, one by one, and was shocked at what she saw—close-up, flash images of a young, unwilling female in various stages of undress, then bruised and beaten...seemingly lifeless. Sue was horrified, stunned. She never expected anything like this. She saved the photos to her computer then closed the folder feeling disgust, fear, and extreme helplessness.

A number of questions popped into her mind. Who took these pictures? And where were they taken? Who was this girl? It wasn't Emily! Did the girl survive, or not? Who would do this to an innocent young girl? Did Emily know these pictures were in the box? Why would the perpetrator keep these photos—as a souvenir? Sue needed to find the answers to all these questions. But where to start? Dan Gilson? Perhaps the magician or the unknown person with the burner phone. It would be a process of elimination unless she could find some additional evidence. Protocol was to have the police dust the thumb drive for fingerprints and test for DNA. But then she thought...

"Maybe I can set a trap..."

27

L ou rang the doorbell at Tristen's house with Sue at his side and was greeted by the parents, Jim and Linda Phillips.

"Good afternoon. I'm Lou Perlo," he said, showing them his identification, "and this is Sue Gainer." Sue nodded.

Linda assumed that it had to do with Tristen and Emily, and it was. "Come on in. I'll get Tristen." She disappeared for a few minutes then returned with a skinny kid who looked a lot younger than his twenty-one years. He was dressed in blue jeans, worn-out sneakers, and a t-shirt with Harry Potter on the front. Since he was an adult, his parents removed themselves while Lou and Sue asked their questions.

"Tristen, this will be a recorded interview." Lou started the recording app on his smartphone. "We know that you've talked to the police already, but would you go over the details of the last time you saw Emily?"

Tristen repeated what he told Detectives Grant and Sills, again leaving out that he tore her shirt. He went through the scene on Emily's street. "Emily told me she was 'moving on' and found someone else, and I was seething mad and jealous."

"Were you angry enough to hurt Emily?"

"No, man. I loved her. I'd do anything to get her back. I thought about fighting the other guy, whoever he was, but he was bigger than me."

Sue spoke up. "Tristen, do you know anything about a wooden box that Emily sold to a guy named Dan Gilson?"

"A box? I have a black box in my magic act," he offered up. "Is that what you're talking about?"

"No, it's more of a wooden sculpture created by a craftsman."

"No. I don't know anything about it." He looked perplexed.

"Okay, don't worry about it," Sue said, dismissing that topic and moving on to another.

"Did you recognize the man who picked up Emily at the Burger Barn?"

"Nope. He looked like he was in his early 30s. Dark hair. Well-built. I think they had oral sex in the Walmart parking lot." He described what he saw.

Lou wasn't surprised about the sex, but he was surprised to hear that Tristen was there. He and Monica had not noticed the truck Tristen was driving when they looked at the video at Walmart.

He asked, "So you followed them to Walmart. Then what did you do?"

"I followed them to the parking lot on South Clinton by the canal. I thought I'd wait until they came back and see where they'd go next. I waited about thirty minutes for Emily, but I never saw her again."

"Were there any other cars parked there when you arrived?"

"There was another pickup truck, but it was empty when I got there. And a car came a few minutes later with a woman driving."

"Did you go on the trail?"

"After the guy Emily was with drove off alone, I went on the trail for about a quarter mile, but I didn't see a single soul, not even the woman walker. I thought Emily might have kept walking, you know? Maybe they had a fight and broke up."

"What kind of vehicle was he driving?"

"Black Ford 150 pickup. Didn't even think to look at the license plate at the time."

"Would you be able to identify him if you saw him again or in a photo?"

"One-hundred percent."

❧ 28 ❧

J ared Poole was cruising down a busy shopping
area in his new white SUV. Stores had just
closed for the night. He revved the engine at the
red light, not only due to his impatience, but just to
be "cool." His vehicle crept closer and closer to the
intersection, waiting for the light to change, and, when
it did, his tires left skid marks on the highway as he
sped away.

Suddenly he spotted blue flashing lights in his
rear-view mirror.

"Shit," he said disgustedly as he pulled over.

The police officer exited his patrol car, marked the
rear of Jared's vehicle with his fingerprints, and
carefully walked up to the open window, with a hand
on his sidearm.

"I'm Officer Michaels. Are you in a big hurry
tonight?" asked the officer, who then briefly spoke in
code into his radio.

"No, sir," Jared remarked with an attitude.

"Do you know why I stopped you?"

"No...sir." Jared made a grimace, wishing this cop
would just go away.

"Well, you sped away from that light pretty fast.
Did you check the intersection first?" He turned on his

torch, shining it inside Jared's car. Being a new car, it was still pristine. Jared did not reply.

The officer continued, "Do you have anything illegal in your car or on your person?"

"No, sir." Jared suddenly remembered the gun in his glove compartment—the *stolen* gun. He could feel perspiration forming on his forehead.

"I need your license and your registration," the officer commanded.

Jared pulled them from his wallet and handed them to the officer, who carried them back to his cruiser and checked the information on his computer.

After returning the credentials, Officer Michaels said, "I'll just give you a warning this time, Mr. Poole. Take it easy out there." He handed Jared a paper warning, making it official.

"Yes, sir," Jared politely said, greatly relieved that his truck wasn't going to be searched. He signaled and carefully pulled away from the curb. He knew he had to be more cautious. This could have spoiled tonight's plan.

It was now or never. He headed to Carrie's house to get his son.

* * * * *

Carrie dozed off watching the 11 o'clock news in the living room, which was on a low volume so it wouldn't disturb the baby's sleep. An unexpected noise startled her awake. In her sleepiness, she felt confused. Did she really hear something or was it part of a dream? She looked around and listened more carefully for a repeat of the sound. It was then that she looked at the doorbell's camera monitor beneath the TV set. In the dim light outside her front door, she could see that there was someone lurking on her porch. It was a shadow-like person, grayed out in the absence of light. The person was wearing a dark hoodie, mask, and skull cap. She took a deep breath in, suddenly frozen to her chair. Regaining some of her sensibilities, she reached for her cell phone on the side table. As she called 911, she heard the sound again—perhaps a key turning in the lock. Even though the key wasn't working, the person kept trying.

Then, the person gave up and left. She eventually heard a police siren nearing her house.

After explaining to one of the officers about the attempted break-in, she showed him the doorbell video. Carrie told him that she couldn't recognize the person, but it might have been her ex who had a key to the old lock. The police cleared the house and searched the yard with a flashlight and advised her to get an order of protection. She said she would, and this time she meant it.

Even though it was late, she called Sue, without even saying hello first.

"Oh my God, Sue! He was here. I'm sure it was Jared I saw on the doorbell camera, but he had a mask on." Carrie rambled on, "It HAD to have been him. No one else except my mother has a key and she has a new key!"

Sue, who was half asleep, interrupted her. "Slow down, Carrie! Tell me exactly what happened."

Carrie told her that she was awakened by hearing the sound of someone attempting to insert a key into the door lock. "It was a scratching sound on metal that woke me up! Then I looked at the little monitor under the TV! That's when I saw the guy, dressed in a mask. Oh, Sue, I was so scared!"

"Did you call the police?"

"Yeah, I called 911 but the guy was gone by the time they showed up. They checked the house and yard and left." Carrie also mentioned the restraining order.

"Do you want to come here for the rest of the night?" Sue offered.

"No. No, I'm okay now. Besides, where would Justin sleep?" I'll be fine," Carrie concluded.

"Okay. Text me tomorrow and we'll get that restraining order."

They said their goodbyes, but neither slept after that.

The next morning, Carrie texted Sue, who agreed to accompany her downtown for the restraining order based upon Jared's earlier assault. Carrie was interviewed by a female officer in the Victims Assistance Center and, after filling out all the required information, was told that, after a court hearing, Jared would not only have to stay away from her and their son, but he could also be arrested if he threatened her or their son in any way. Carrie prayed that it would discourage Jared and not incense him.

* * * * *

When Jared left Carrie's doorway, his reaction to the new locks on Carrie's doors had been one of anger and frustration. He had hoped to carry out his plan of sneaking inside and taking his son, by gunpoint if necessary. But, after trying his key several times, he realized that she had changed the locks. The curtains had been closed but he saw the flickering light of the television. Jared could have banged on the door, but he knew that she'd just call the cops. He'd have to come up with another plan later, and he wasn't going to stick around in case the police were on the way.

He felt the security of the gun in his waistband then went back to his SUV.

As he drove away, he thought about everything she did, making him more and more angry. His patience was wearing thin. He was getting desperate.

29

After making sure Carrie was safe, it was time for Sue to discuss the contents of the thumb drive with Lou.

"This is just sick. He is definitely a predator," Lou warned, shaking his head. "We need to get this guy."

Sue explained her plan to trap the killer. Lou paused before replying.

"You realize how dangerous this is, don't you? And I'm going to be asked why we didn't follow protocol and let the police handle this. It puts me in a bad spot...but... I admit it's an interesting way to bag the killer." Lou sat back in his chair and looked at Sue. He finally yielded and allowed Sue to give it a try. "This is our only chance. If it doesn't work, we have to call Chief Mulroney."

"Agreed," Sue relented.

A few minutes later, Sue was on her way to Dan Gilson's house.

Dan watched her from his window and wondered what the P.I. wanted now. At least she was alone and posed less of a threat, but he was prepared to react if she became aggressive towards him. But then what?

On second thought, he decided to play nice—at least in the beginning.

He walked out of the house to confront her, inserting the screwdriver in the pocket of his deep overalls.

"Forget something?" Dan asked, checking Sue out from head to toe. It didn't appear that she was packing.

Sue thought about her training and was ready if he made a threatening move. "I need to ask you a favor."

Dan reacted with surprise and suspicion. There was no response, but she continued. "I brought your box back but I want you to put it where someone can easily steal it."

"What? You want someone to break into my garage and steal it?"

"We'll do our best to get it back to you, but if it gets destroyed or lost, we'll refund your seventy-five dollars."

His brows furrowed. "What's this all about, anyway?" His lip was twitching.

"Trust me, Mr. Gilson—this one time. We need to find Emily Rogers' killer. We think... no, *I know,* this box is connected to the crime. What do you think? Will you let this play out?"

The one reassuring thought Dan had was that they did not appear to suspect him, and that was a relief. Unless this was a trick. He debated it in his mind, finally willing to take the chance.

"Well, alright," he said begrudgingly.

"Great. I've wiped it clean of fingerprints, but I would like you to take it out of the backseat of my car and place it on your garage shelf, where you had it before. We know that your prints are in the system already and we can eliminate them when we recover the box...if my plan works. Don't lock your garage for the next few nights. Put an ad for the box online but if someone comes snooping, *please,* do not confront the person. Let them steal the box."

Still suspicious, Dan asked, "What if they steal my tools?"

"This person will only be interested in the box, I assure you."

"You'd better damned be right," Dan warned with a bit of a growl.

Sue added, "Oh, one other thing."

"What's that?"

"Whatever you do, don't open the box."

⚘ 30 ⚘

Katie Winslow woke up with the sun shining directly in her eyes. She groaned and turned to one side. She vaguely recalled seeing a man in her bed, but he wasn't there now, although she went through the motions of feeling the sheets where he apparently slept. Was it a dream? She opened her eyes, and instantly regretted it. She had a *huge* headache. Naked, she stood up next to the bed, holding the padded headboard for support. She felt pain everywhere. She slowly made her way to the bathroom and saw herself in the mirror.

"Oh, shit!" she exclaimed at her appearance.

It wasn't just the typical hangover "look"; she had bruises on her abdomen and upper arms, and clear bite marks on her breasts and thighs. And her vagina hurt and that made it difficult to walk. The worst part was that she didn't remember any of it—just a vague recollection that a man had been in her bed.

After peeing, which burned as it dribbled into the toilet bowl, she leaned over and barfed into a waste basket. She just pushed it aside. She really needed to shower and brush her teeth, but she knew that the way she felt and the horrific way she looked was not normal. If only she could remember what happened the night before!

She recalled going to the local bar to meet friends, but she didn't think any of them showed up. There was a guy she didn't know... He bought her a drink... Next thing she knew, it was morning.

Katie started trembling. She thought, *"I had to have been raped! Why can't I remember anything? What if he put something in my drink? Oh my God, he knows where I live!"* It scared her. Without even brushing her hair, she got into a sweat suit and called for a Lyft ride to take her to the hospital.

The electronic doors automatically opened as Katie entered the Emergency Room.

"Can I help you?" asked the attentive black nurse behind the desk.

"I think I was raped," Katie claimed, keeping her voice low. "I can't remember." She furrowed her eyebrows and shook her head in confusion.

The nurse immediately called for assistance, and within a minute, Katie was on a gurney being wheeled into a curtained area. She looked away in shame. It was hurtful to think that she allowed this to happen. Did she? Katie started crying and a different nurse handed her a small box of tissues.

"It'll be alright, honey," the new nurse said. "We're going to move you to a private room as soon as it's available. We had to call the police. You were very smart to come to the hospital."

Katie nodded okay, and soon they began to push her bed out of the ER.

A little later, Major Crimes Detective Kim DeVries came in and had a forensic nurse collect a rape kit, and scrape the inside of her fingernails, take her fingerprints, and capture images of her body where she had been brutalized. After the nurse was done, DeVries assured Katie, "You're safe now. I will do my best to find the person who did this to you."

Detective DeVries was also interested in the facts— whatever Katie could remember from the night before.

Katie related what she remembered, while DeVries took notes. The rape took place in Katie's own apartment. Kim asked for her house key, which Katie supplied from her purse.

Back at headquarters, DeVries submitted the kit knowing that rape kits were lower on the priority list than murder evidence. She also requested that the DNA be run against their database, while she went to Katie's apartment with two members of the crime-scene team to look for additional evidence.

The investigative team dusted the doorknob for fingerprints but didn't find anything other than Katie's prints. Everything seemed to be wiped clean or handled with gloves. *"Who would wear gloves if they planned to have sex? Not a normal person!"* Kim thought. The apartment was clean and organized, but DeVries noticed a putrid smell. Immediately, she knew that Katie had vomited, so she directed that it be collected and analyzed to identify what was in Katie's stomach. They took the sheets off the bed and bagged them. It might take a while for them to be tested.

Katie was discharged after her wounds were treated. Terrified to be in her apartment alone, she locked the door and slid the slide bolt across the door frame. Katie noticed that the police took her linens. She'd never sleep on those sheets again, anyway. She showered until the hot water ran out and cried the whole time. Katie then called her best friend Julie and begged to stay at her place until she found a new apartment. Julie was shocked to hear what had happened to her friend and agreed to let her share her small, one-bedroom apartment.

That was only the beginning of Katie's trauma. What followed were the night terrors—frightening nightmares that made her scream out, night after night.

"I want to die!" she confessed to her friend, weeping. "Please, just let me die."

Putting her arm around Katie, Julie calmly responded, "We're going to get you through this. We'll find out who did this and make sure he goes to prison, if it's the last thing I do."

❧ 31 ❧

Gary Alan Ritter was an invisible guy. An extremely intelligent, invisible guy. Yes, he had a wife and two children and a well-paying job at the University of Rochester. But he was so invisible that only his boss called him by his first name; no one else recognized him by any name. If he passed someone in the hallway, they would walk right on by, not noticing him in his starched white lab coat and black-rimmed glasses. When he worked on a project, he looked just like everyone else who worked in the labs—white coat and an eye on his microscope. If he was out sick or on vacation, no one really missed him, but the payroll people knew the name and how many vacation and sick days he had left. They just never knew who he was.

He had a daily exercise regimen and was quite a strong man, but no one ever noticed his muscles under the lab coat. Working out was an escape from the long, hard days at his job—a job that was tedious and strictly enforced by government regulations and medical practices and guidelines. Gary never complained, though. He always did what was expected of him.

Despite all this, Gary was a caring human being. He loved all people, rich and poor, fat and thin, young and old, ugly and beautiful. He felt great emotion for those who were ill and couldn't help themselves, especially the elderly and the young children who spent endless months in institutions or hospitals with diseases that were difficult to cure, if not impossible. He donated blood and platelets several times a year, and once he even donated his bone marrow. He also wrote a big check every year for the Golisano Children's Hospital in Rochester. He never expected anything in return—no words of gratitude, no plaques or awards, no publicity, not even a free donut and a cup of coffee. He was just happy being Gary, doing what Gary does.

His wife Maryann was an interior decorator by trade, but she chose to take a break from full-time employment to raise their two children and make the home comfortable and beautiful for her family. She was active at the children's grammar school by volunteering in the library and cafeteria and she helped sew costumes and build sets for the annual school play. Like her husband, she loved to help people. Unlike her husband, she was well known and well liked in the community. She was always visible and everyone knew her by sight and by name.

Gary and Maryann had their two children later in life than some people. Their first priority was to get their degrees and establish themselves in their jobs, then start a family. It worked out well for them and for the children, who were just as intelligent as their parents and destined for great things in life.

Then, in one day, everything changed.

Suddenly, everyone in the city of Rochester, the town of Brighton where they lived, and everyone in all of Western New York found out who Gary was.

He was a killer.

The word spread like wildfire. The newspaper, four local television stations, radio shows, and every resident's social media page was inundated with the name Gary Alan Ritter. His name became the top name searched on the Internet. National television shows sent crews to film hour-long documentaries on his crimes, showing his face on every TV screen in America.

The worst part was the notoriety. The children were bullied and had to be pulled from their school immediately. Local reporters were stationed on their street with cameras rolling, their large trucks driving over the well-maintained lawn with wheels spinning in the sod. Neighbors were suspicious of the entire family and a few began throwing eggs at their once-lovely home and posting signs telling them to leave. The shame was unbearable. Maryann took the two children and went to her mom's house in Syracuse. It was no longer safe to be at home and she no longer trusted Gary to be with his kids. And, of course, Gary was now in jail, this time wearing an orange jumpsuit, looking just like every other prisoner.

ꙮ 32 ꙮ

Monica burst into Lou's office. Startled, he looked up at the excited expression on her face.

"They caught him!" she exclaimed.

"They caught...?"

"The Canal Killer!"

"What? Who did they arrest?"

"Some guy in his 40s, lives in Brighton. According to the news report, they found his DNA at both murders!"

Lou did a search on his computer browser and read the breaking news story:

"Gary Alan Ritter was arrested today and charged in the murders of teenagers Emily Rogers and Sarah Bennington, who were both strangled and whose bodies were found in the canal recently. Ritter vehemently denies both murders. Police claim they have an air-tight case. 'DNA don't lie,' said Detective Crandall of the Rochester Police Department when asked about the two young women who were murdered. Police would not make any additional comment about these cases."

"Kelsey!" Lou shouted. Kelsey scrambled to his door, and Sue wasn't far behind. They both knew something was up.

"Police arrested a Gary Alan Ritter in the Rogers murder. See what you can find on him," he ordered.

Sue asked, "Did he drive a dark pickup truck?"

Lou shook his head. "Doesn't say anything about a vehicle."

Kelsey responded, "I'll find out what kind of car he has." She ran back to her desk and started typing in her search topics.

Ten minutes later, she had what she needed for Lou.

"Caucasian. 45. Went to St. John Fisher and got a B.S. in Biology. Employed by the University of Rochester. Lives in Brighton. Drives a Toyota Avalon Hybrid. Never owned a pickup truck. Family guy. Married, two kids. No social media accounts."

Sue looked perplexed. "This doesn't feel right to me."

"Well, they say they found his DNA. Sounds like an open-and-shut case," Monica stated.

"Why is his DNA in the system?" Sue asked. "There has to be something more."

Kelsey went back to her computer. This time she searched through newspaper articles and other public records.

While she was busy, Lou spoke up. "I'll call Deputy Chief Mulroney at the RPD to see if he'll tell me more, like what proof they have on him." Lou hit the keypad numbers on his phone and put it on "speaker."

"Mulroney," the voice said.

"Hi, Sean. Lou Perlo here."

"Lou! How are you?"

"Good thanks. And you?"

"Doing well, thanks. What is it you need from me?" He anticipated Lou's inquiry.

"What can you tell me about this Ritter guy? I was hired by the Rogers family to look into Emily's disappearance."

"Can't say much about the case right now, but we have solid DNA on him. It was on the earbud wires found in Brighton and a pair of women's prescription sunglasses we found near the Gates crime scene, which we now know belonged to Sarah Bennington."

"I understand he denies everything."

"That's what he says, but we say differently. We'll get a confession when we confirm other evidence and hear possible witness testimony," Mulroney added confidently.

"Was there any evidence in his vehicle?"

"Negative. We went over it with a fine-toothed comb. He may have used someone else's vehicle. That's a possibility. Our detectives still have some work to do."

"Okay, thanks. Let me know if there's anything new you can share with me."

"Will do."

They cut the call.

Lou looked at his team. "Well, they have him dead-to-rights with DNA. Unless we can prove otherwise, Ritter is going down for these murders, and maybe deservedly so."

Kelsey returned to Lou's office. "Okay. Found something," she said breathlessly.

They all stared at her, waiting for the update.

"When he was in college, there was a suspicious death in the off-campus housing unit where he lived.

The police used buccal swabs on everyone. They ruled Gary out, but his DNA remained in the system."

"That's interesting. Was it a crime? Was anyone arrested?"

"Ruled an 'unattended death,'" Kelsey informed them.

They all looked at each other. "That's weird! It could have been caused by pretty much anything!" Sue thought aloud.

They considered that for a moment.

Sue said, "I'm going to the first crime scene. Maybe there's something...anything..."

Lou nodded his agreement. She took off immediately.

She hadn't been to the Trolley Boulevard crime scene before. The entire area was unfamiliar to her. She could hear and see the cars speeding down the 390 expressway on the newly constructed bridge over the road. The canal looked oddly situated in the industrial area of town by today's purpose, but back in its heyday, the canal was created for trade.

Motor vehicles were blocked from entering the trailway, so Sue parked her SUV in the nearest parking area and got out. She looked for surveillance cameras. Some of the local businesses had to have some. Once on the trail, she noticed the large railroad trestle nearby. She walked about a quarter mile in both directions, looking for anything that might help to finger the Ritter guy or to clear him. But Sue found nothing.

Instead of getting on the expressway back to the office, Sue drove casually down one of the most traveled roads, which had back-to-back car dealers.

Sue had a hunch. What if the killer got rid of his vehicle after the last murder? Finding a black Ford 150 pickup truck in a used-car lot seemed like an impossible undertaking, but Monica and Lou mentioned that the vehicle in question had damage to the front end when they reviewed the Walmart surveillance. It wouldn't be that difficult to narrow them down.

She drove to the farthest used-car dealer and worked her way back towards the city. Lot after lot, no damaged pickups were found. Sue was exhausted and decided to resume the next day. If that didn't work out, perhaps Lou would have another idea.

❧ 33 ❧

Mrs. Gainer had a pot roast in the oven when Sue arrived home.

"Mmm. Smells divine! I'm starving!"

"Can you set the table for me?" Carol asked.

Sue washed up then set the table for three, using china that had been in the family for three generations. The white linen tablecloth was also an heirloom from her maternal grandmother. It was well kept and still looked new, although not exactly in style.

"Your dad's not eating much, but he wants to join us," Carol quietly mentioned.

The thought of her dad losing more weight was upsetting. She hoped he'd gain some of it back when chemo was done.

Dinner conversation turned to the latest news. "I heard they finally caught the Canal Killer," Jerry said, relieved that his daughter would now be safe when she jogged.

"Thank God," Carol inserted. "Who would have thought that a bio-chemist from the University of Rochester was a murderer?"

"I didn't know him," Jerry added. "I thought I knew everybody!"

Sue just kept on eating. She didn't want to put in her two cents since it was her opinion that the police had the wrong man. She had no proof, though. The meal finished up with peach cobbler, a family favorite.

When the phone rang, she was relieved to excuse herself from the table.

"Sue, this is Officer, er, Chris Williams."

"Hi, Chris!" Sue surmised that he was calling about the arrest.

"Hope I'm calling at a good time."

"Yes, we just finished dinner."

"I just wanted you to know that the canal path is safe again."

"I heard they arrested someone."

"Yes. So, I'm wondering if you might like to go out for dinner tomorrow night. I'm off duty."

"Oh!" The invitation took her by surprise. She hesitated for a moment, then replied, "That would be very nice. What time?"

"How about if I pick you up at six?"

"Sounds good." They said their goodbyes and ended the call.

Sue went back to the table. "I've got a date tomorrow!"

"Oh?" her parents said in unison.

"Officer Williams from the BPD!"

"Wow, I'm happy for you," her mom sincerely replied, looking pleased.

Her dad had to have the last word. "Just as long as you're home by midnight."

Sue laughed. Of course, he was joking. Or was he? She chuckled all the way up to her bedroom. But she thought, *"I need to get an apartment!"*

❧ 34 ❧

Chris Williams dressed in a dark, tight-fitting polo shirt that displayed his generous upper arm muscles and a pair of faded blue jeans and drove to Sue's house in his Mazda to pick her up for their first date. He knew he had to go through the ritual of meeting her parents. Chris shook their hands as he was introduced. There were no glaring looks from her dad or biting lips on her mom. They trusted him because he was a police officer and sworn to protect and serve.

"Have a good time," Carol wished them as they headed for his car. She turned to Jerry, "At least we don't have to worry about this one." He nodded his agreement while closing the door.

"Where are we going to go?" Sue asked Chris.

"I thought we'd go out for some Italian food, have a glass of wine, relax," Chris said as he opened the passenger door for Sue.

"Sounds great," she replied as she slipped in her seat, hoping there'd be a kiss at the end of the night.

The restaurant was cozy and warm, heavy with the aroma of sauce, basil, and garlic. They were led to a corner table, on which a candle was newly lit, and handed large menus. The waiter immediately brought over a dish of herbed olive oil and a small loaf of sliced bread to enjoy before they made their meal decisions.

Sue decided on Chicken French—a Rochester specialty—and a glass of Riesling. Chris went for the lasagna and passed on the wine, having a Genny beer instead.

"You look beautiful tonight," Chris told Sue, who was wearing a short white top that showed a bit of midriff and a long, flowered skirt.

"Thank you. You look...great...too," she responded, looking at his muscular build. They smiled at each other, attempting to read each other's mind.

Trying not to use his interrogation voice, Chris asked her about her life, relationships, and jobs, and Sue replied willingly, although there wasn't much to say about relationships. He reached out and put his hand on hers and it felt warm and welcoming. She was relaxed and having a good time and asked him similar questions. Chris had never been married, but he had dated several women. They didn't work out. Most of them wanted a husband with an 8 to 5 job and he couldn't promise that.

After dinner, they returned to the car, and Chris drove by his house in a quiet neighborhood on the east side of town. It was a two-story brick-and-stucco house with a small front yard.

"This is where I live. It just takes a few minutes to get to work and it's convenient to stores and restaurants," he informed her. "Want to come in for a drink?"

Slightly nervous about going into a strange man's house, Sue hesitated.

"I don't bite," he said, smiling.

"Sure. Why not?" Sue relented.

He showed her around the clean but outdated kitchen, small dining room, and cozy living room with a pair of built-in bookcases next to the fireplace. She sat on a loveseat as Chris opened a bottle of wine and poured two glasses, handing one to her.

"Thanks," Sue purred.

He sat down next to her, leaving very little room between them. They tapped each other's glass and Chris said, "To us!"

Sue smiled and repeated, "To us." He took a sip of wine and so did Sue, then the glasses were placed on coasters on the coffee table. He put an arm around her shoulder.

"So," Chris started, "why did you agree to go out with me tonight?"

Sue thought it was a slightly strange question and felt she was dealing with a strong ego here, but she decided to tell the truth. Looking into his eyes, she smiled. "Well, you're very handsome and you have a nice smile." She smirked then paused. "And I'm interested in police work and I was hoping that I could pick your brain on occasion in my new job as a P.I."

Chris moved closer. "Is that really why you came tonight?" His breathing was heavy, and she could feel his breath and his lips near her ear, then kissing it.

Sue stuttered, as she was starting to get very warm, "Well, I...I have to admit that I'm a bit turned on right now." Her throat was dry. Her heart was beating faster.

He inched even closer, if that was possible. "Mmm. Oh, yeah? Tell me. How turned on are you?" Without giving her a chance to reply, he put his arms around her and kissed her long and hard. His hands reached for her breast, as she put her hands on the back of his strong neck. After several minutes of kisses and fondling, he gently broke the embrace.

"Come with me," Chris said, pulling her up from the sofa. He took her hand and led her to the stairway.

"Uh, Chris, I'm not sure I... I don't think I should..."

"No?" He sounded a bit disappointed. "We're both adults. I'll be gentle." He pulled her tight to his body, kissing her again, perhaps trying to make her change her mind. It did tempt her.

"I need a little more time," Sue gently protested, hoping that's as far as it would go tonight.

"Okay, Sue. We'll give it more time." He unwillingly loosened his hold on her.

Sue breathed a sigh of relief, with a tinge of regret. She really enjoyed the thought of him making love to her, and she really, really wanted to see his body. And feel his body. And see his gorgeous body on top of hers. And experience the excitement of lovemaking. So, why was she so hesitant? She didn't know. It just wasn't time.

After they finished their wine, he drove her to her parents' house and gave her a kiss goodnight in the car. She said she'd see him soon and then got out of the passenger side. As Sue walked to her front door, she heard his tires squeal when he left the curb, as if in anger. Her body stiffened as she watched his car go down the street, leaving her feeling disturbed.

In the safety of her little bedroom, she sat on the edge of her bed, petting Butterscotch, and wondered if she had made a mistake.

∾ 35 ∾

When the for-sale post for the carved box appeared on the "Buy and Sell" site, Rich couldn't believe his luck. The description read, "Unique craftsman piece. Fine maple and cherry woodwork." Emily sold it for seventy-five dollars but the price was now one-hundred dollars. Not only did the seller have a "Reply" button for responses and offers, but he also included his complete name and address.

Rich couldn't risk losing the box again, so he began to make plans to retrieve it. And he didn't want to pay for it. After all, it was *his* box and Emily had no right to sell it.

Besides, Emily told him that the dude was a pervert. She didn't think that Rich had listened to her, but he had. Dan Gilson had sexually molested Emily and, although he and Emily had had a disagreement afterward, Rich wanted some revenge on this guy. He just didn't know anything else about him except that he was old. Old can be "aged," or old can be thirty to a teenager. So, Rich had to think out his plan carefully.

Dressing in all black—a turtleneck shirt, pants, sneakers, gloves, and ski mask—Rich wanted to be a shadow in the night. He carried some burglary tools and a flashlight. He also slipped a gun into his waistband, just in case.

The night was very warm and he was overdressed for the weather. He began sweating profusely. It was just a nuisance, though, and something he couldn't worry about.

He drove his vehicle and parked it a block from Dan's house. He walked the rest of the way, darting through yards and hopping fences. He was thankful that he was strong and fit.

When he arrived at Dan's property, he hid in the bushes next to the shed for at least 15 minutes, watching and waiting for any sign of activity. The door to Dan's garage appeared to be open. There were no vehicles inside—just a table saw, various pieces of lumber, and a lot of sawdust on the floor. Rich wasn't sure whether Dan planned to come out and close the garage door before bed or if he just wouldn't bother. Rich didn't want to be caught red-handed.

It was quite silent during his wait. Rich could hear the "croakers" in a nearby pond and occasional road traffic. There was a barking dog in the distance.

A television flickered inside Dan's house. Rich didn't see any curtain movement or shadowed figures. He had to wait until Dan went to sleep to approach the house. Rich's plan was to silently cut a hole in the window of the back door and slip his arm inside and unlock it. Then, with his flashlight, he would search for the box without waking up Gilson. Rich hoped Dan was a heavy sleeper; he'd listen for his snoring. He also hoped the box was not in the dude's bedroom. If Dan confronted him, he might have to use his gun. He really didn't want to attract any attention from the neighbors or deal with an angry man, much less shoot him. But if he had to, he would.

Suddenly, the TV was turned off, leaving the house pitch dark. Rich continued to wait until the time felt right.

Thirty minutes later, he silently approached the garage. He used his flashlight and saw the interior door to the house at the far end of the garage. There were no windows in the door to cut. He had a moment of complete discouragement as he tried to decide on a Plan B. He flashed the light around the garage.

Then he saw it. The wooden box, sitting on a shelf! His heart was beating out of his chest as he went over to the shelf, being careful not to disturb the stack of wood underneath. "Damn!" he whispered under his mask, feeling excitement. He couldn't believe his luck!

Carrying the oddly shaped box back to his vehicle was more difficult, as Rich couldn't hop over fences the way he arrived. He had to walk out in the road and hoped that cars wouldn't pass him by, seeing him with the evidence. He was lucky not to see a single soul.

When he got to his vehicle, he whipped off his sweaty mask, opened the door, and carefully placed the box on the passenger seat. Silently, the mask fell on the grass without notice. But Rich had what he came for—the prize inside this most curious box.

* * * * *

Dan Gilson heard a slight noise in his garage as he rested in bed with a warm breeze coming through the window screen. He waited until it was quiet again before he walked into the garage. The box was gone. Just like that private investigator expected.

* * * * *

Rich returned to his house. Without noticing that he had tracked in a fair amount of sawdust from his boots, he shed his clothing and threw them into the washer. He was missing his ski mask. He checked his vehicle, but the mask was nowhere to be found. Rich did not want to look for it in Dan's neighborhood in the light of day and be noticed or recognized, so he just dismissed it. Hopefully, it was on the highway somewhere.

He sat down at the kitchen table and, with a quick motion of two thumbs and a twist, he opened the box. There was his thumb drive, still in place. He breathed a sigh of relief. He walked over to his computer and put the drive into a port. The folder "Trolley" popped up. Rich waited a moment then double-clicked on the folder.

When he saw the thumbnail icons of the photos, he became confused at first. When he switched to larger images, his heart dropped.

"WHAT THE FUCK?" he screamed as he skimmed through the photos. "SON OF A BITCH!" He smashed a fist on the table, jostling everything on top.

There on his screen were several photos of an orange cat rolling in catnip.

36

The morning after the wooden box was stolen, the local police, crime technicians, and Sue Gainer arrived at Dan Gilson's house, with the intent of looking for evidence in and around his garage.

His house was immediately cleared and Dan was checked for weapons before the police allowed the technicians to begin processing the site. Dan was ordered to stay inside his house while the team investigated. The ex-con was uneasy to have police nosing around his garage, shed, and property, but he was more than happy to sequester himself in the house. He opened a non-alcoholic beer and sat at his kitchen table waiting for the police to leave.

After an hour of dusting for fingerprints, the only prints they found were Dan's. The sawdust on the floor was disturbed but there were no recognizable footprints. They expanded their search for clues to the shed, around the fences, and even into the street. No rock was left unturned.

Suddenly there was a shout from one of the detectives. "Over here!" He was standing in the grass near the curb a few houses down the street.

Sue, another detective, and a crime-scene technician walked over to him.

"A black ski mask," he pointed out.

Photos were taken and then the hat was placed in a plastic bag, which was then sealed and marked. It would be tested for contact DNA. There were also traces of sawdust in the same area, connecting it to the crime scene.

This was just what Sue had been praying for—evidence! She was hopeful that it would come back to this unknown "Rich" guy, whoever he really was, assuming his DNA was in the system. Now, it was just a matter of waiting on the crime lab to do its job.

As the investigative team disbanded, Dan stared out the window and watched them pack up and leave. Once again, he was free to use his saw and other tools, but there was fingerprint powder everywhere that had to be cleaned up. He looked around disgustedly. It would be the last time he'd ever agree to some "cockamamie, harebrained" idea of some "damn female," involving the police. He just wanted to be left alone. Forever.

He went back inside to his desk, pulled out the middle drawer, and felt the paper taped to the bottom. He pulled it off and looked at it. It was a photo from social media of that girl Emily wearing a crop top in the thinnest material, showing her protruding nipples and the silver ring piercing in her belly button. He grinned, remembering how soft her skin felt. Yes, indeed. He remembered very well.

⤷ 37 ⤸

Detective Steve Grant stared at the lab results from the ski mask found near Dan Gilson's house the night of the break-in. It was puzzling to say the least. He wondered if there had been a mistake. He called over to the lockup to make sure Gary Ritter was still incarcerated. He was.

"How is this possible?" he asked as he showed the profile to his fellow detectives. It showed that the contact DNA from the ski mask came back to Gary Ritter.

Grant called Lou Perlo and gave him the news, and Lou told Sue. The two of them sat in Lou's office trying to figure out how this could have happened.

Sue asked, "Could Gary's son have his dad's DNA? Or maybe he dropped his dad's hat there and stole the box."

Lou dismissed both. "He's what—12 years old?"

"Maybe the hat has been there several days. Maybe Gary knows Dan Gilson," Sue proposed.

Lou concluded, "I think the police need to talk to Gary Ritter."

Detective Grant had the same idea and invited Sue to watch the interview on a monitor in the next room.

* * * * *

Gary Ritter was escorted into the interview room wearing his orange jumpsuit and sat down at the table with his hands in cuffs.

Detectives Grant and Sills entered the room. "Hi, Gary. Remember us?" Grant asked.

"Yes," he said. No more, no less. He pushed up the black-rimmed glasses on his nose.

"Good. We have a few more questions for you," he paused as he looked over his notes. "By any chance, do you have a twin brother?"

Gary shook his head. "No."

"Do you own a black ski mask?"

"Maybe. I do ski in the winter and sometimes I wear a knitted hat when I shovel snow. I *think* it's black. It may be dark blue."

"Do you know where that hat is?"

"At home in the closet by the garage," Gary revealed. "What's this about, anyway?"

"Does your son ever wear your hat?"

"My son is living in Syracuse. You'd have to ask him."

"Did you instruct anyone to use your hat to steal a box from Dan Gilson?"

"Who? I don't know anyone by that name."

"Is there anyone who has a grudge against you and would have left your hat at a crime scene to finger you?"

"No! What are you talking about? You got the wrong man! I haven't committed any crime! I never killed anyone, especially a teenage girl I never met..."

"Take him back to jail," Grant ordered his deputy. The deputy motioned the prisoner to stand up.

Gary struggled a bit and kept yelling back to the detective that he was innocent, until the elevator door closed and the room was again silent. Grant didn't believe him for a second.

But how did his DNA get on the ski mask? And how did the ski mask end up on Dan's road? He needed answers or the entire case against Ritter might be dismissed.

❧ 38 ❧

The hot summer sun beat down on Sue's black SUV as she sat in her shorts on hot black leather car seats waiting for Marvin LaDue to appear outside of his run-down city house.

"I should have gotten a tan SUV with fabric seats; maybe these darn seats wouldn't be so hot!" Sue complained to herself. *"And maybe I shouldn't have worn shorts!"* One thigh was pulled off the leather upholstery, then the other. "Yow!" she cried and sat back down. After checking in the back seat to see if she had something to put between herself and the leather, she gave up and focused on the job ahead.

During this surveillance, the much wiser P.I. did not plan to tail Mr. LaDue and be caught like the last time. Instead, the house across the street from Marvin was unoccupied and she conveniently parked her vehicle between the two houses, facing Marvin's. The problem was that there was no air flow. Sue didn't want to keep the car running with the air conditioner going, but she did turn it on now and then just to keep from passing out.

"This surveillance stuff is harder than I expected," Sue thought. Opening the large, covered cup of pop in her cupholder, she discovered that all the ice was melted. She took a sip on her straw, just for something

to wet her mouth and occupy her time. As most women do, she hoped that she wouldn't have to find a restroom for a while.

About forty-five minutes later, Sue watched as a delivery driver carried a cardboard box to Marvin's porch. Her digital camera was ready with its telephoto lens. She opened the car windows to get a clear shot if and when Marvin came out.

A few minutes after the delivery man left, Marvin opened his front door and quickly peered into the small black mailbox attached to his siding, but there was no mail. He looked down and spotted the package, then glanced up and down the street to ensure there were no spies. He didn't appear to notice Sue sweltering in her SUV directly across the street.

Marvin stepped out on the porch and picked up the box. Sue's camera snapped picture after picture until Marvin went back inside and shut his door.

"Gotcha," Sue said quietly, as she smirked. Despite her success, she continued to watch his house. This time she wanted to make sure that she had plenty of images for the insurance company. After saving the photos to the "cloud" through her iPhone, Sue put the phone back in her purse.

Feeling confident that she got some good shots, she turned on the air and was about to close her windows. But when she looked up, there were three tall, young men, dressed in shorts and no shirts, standing in front of her car, looking somewhat threatening. One approached the open driver's side window.

"What have we got here? Are you a cop? Hey, look at this!" The other two men went to the passenger side and looked in at the camera and lens on the seat. She could almost see the dollar signs in their eyes. If she didn't react soon, she figured that the agency's equipment would end up in a pawn shop.

Sue thought about her training. She looked at their hands and their waistbands. She didn't see any weapons. One man had his hands on her car door through the open window. Although she didn't know their intentions—it could just be curiosity as to why she was parked there—they were just too close for comfort. She put the car in "drive" and stepped on the gas. All three men were knocked out of the way but no one fell or was injured. One guy had his right hand on the camera when she took off. The moving car made him drop the camera back inside the car. Sue heard some swearing as she drove off.

She sped out into the road, swerving and narrowly missing another car whose driver laid on the horn. Marvin came out to look at what was going on and Sue saw him out of the corner of her eye. No crutches. "Damn!" Sue swore as she drove off.

When Sue arrived back at the office, she examined the camera. She wasn't sure if it was broken or not. She hated facing Lou with the news, but she had no choice.

"Hey, Lou," she greeted her boss.

"How'd it go today?"

"Well, I got some good shots." Sue showed him the photos on her phone, one by one, until he viewed all of them. "I can send them to you and you can pass them along to the insurance company."

Lou looked at her closely. "You sound hesitant. Did Mr. LaDue catch you again?"

"No. Nothing like that." Sue paused. "But I did have a run-in with some tough-looking guys who had their hands on my equipment then dropped it." She showed him the camera, which she had been holding behind her back.

"Uh oh. Let me take a look." He pulled out the SD card and pushed it back in. "Looks okay so far." Then he tried to take a picture. It didn't work. "Hmm, I think it bit the dust. We can file an insurance claim. You'll just have some paperwork to fill out. See Kelsey." He removed the SD card again and handed it to Sue. "Secure the images."

"Okay. Thanks, Lou. Sorry about the camera."

"Well, it happens. As long as you're okay."

"I am."

"Good. I'll have another assignment for you soon. This time it'll be you and Maxim and no major equipment. Meanwhile, get back to the Emily Rogers case."

Her heart skipped a beat at the mention of Maxim. "Got it." Sue left his office and went to see Kelsey who located an insurance form for her to complete.

⤖ 39 ⤖

Sue and Maxim had over an hour to kill before their follow-up meeting with Lou.

They had been on a new investigation, as a couple, taking videos of a man who was accused of cheating on his wife. They followed the man to a restaurant where he planned to meet a young brunette woman for lunch. Maxim and Sue went into the restaurant and sat at the table next to the man. Maxim pressed a finger on a digital spy camera discreetly magnetized to his metal shirt button, as Sue asked the waiter for a glass of water to start the video recording.

The brunette they were expecting arrived on time.

"Carla, I'm so glad you could come," the man said politely as he stood for her and pulled out a chair.

Sue thought, *"Nice guy—so far!"*

They chatted briefly about their jobs, and then got serious.

"Mike, have you asked your wife for that divorce?"

"Not yet. But I will, don't worry."

"I can't wait too long. I'm already starting to show!"

Sue's eyes opened wide to hear that the woman, Carla, was pregnant!

"I know, I know. I'll do it this weekend. You sure you don't want an abortion?" he inquired sheepishly.

"No!" The woman was adamant.

Sue thought, *"Well, he just failed the nice-guy test."*

"Okay, okay. I'm sure she'll throw me out when I tell her. I assume I can move in with you. Right?"

"Yes. I'll need your help taking care of the baby," she informed him in no uncertain terms.

No reply, but the man sat back in his chair, looking defeated. Sue imagined that it was not what he wanted his new life with Carla to be like. Instead of sex and adoration, he'd be changing diapers.

Sue continued to record their conversations through lunch. The couple walked out and kissed before parting ways. Sue had a flashback to her former employer, who fell in love with a married man. At least she wasn't pregnant!

Sue and Max also left the restaurant, leaving a tip on the table for the waiter's service. They jumped into the Perlo company car.

"We got all of it," Sue said happily.

"It's a great video, too!" Maxim reported. "All in a day's work, I guess."

"So," Sue started to say. "What should we do now? We have over an hour to kill."

"Leave it to me," he said with a grin as he pulled away from the curb.

In a few minutes they were in a rural area south of the city, perhaps the foothills of the Bristol Mountains, as the road was hilly. The sun was bright in the blue sky with just an occasional cloud. Maxim made a quick left onto a dirt road that led to the top of a small hill and alongside a cornfield, out of sight to anyone on the busy road below.

"A cornfield?" Sue looked at him as if he were crazy.

He opened the windows and turned off the car. A summer breeze gently lifted wisps of Sue's blonde hair.

They kissed, with each kiss lasting longer than the kiss before. It was getting hot in the car in more ways than one.

"Excuse me," Maxim said as he opened his driver's side door and stepped out. He carefully dismantled the spy camera and pulled off his shirt, which made Sue grin with pleasure, noting his fine abs. Then he began to remove his trousers! Sue's chin dropped, wondering where this was going. It didn't take long to find out, as he wasn't wearing boxers or briefs!

He gleefully ran around to her side of the car, with everything exposed and, um, in her face—naked as a jaybird and loving every minute of it. She laughed out loud at his antics. He then opened her door, pulled her out, and started taking her clothes off.

"What are you doing? Are you nuts?" she squealed. Her clothes were thrown into the front seat of the car.

Soon they were both standing naked in the cornfield, except for their slip-on shoes. He kissed her, holding her body tight to his, his strong arms surrounding her. She could feel his manhood get hard against her. After several kisses, he opened the rear passenger door and asked her to get in. They found a way to make the most of an hour...

As they were both breathing heavily and feeling remnants of a lingering climax, they sat up and gently kissed twice.

"I love you, Sue."

"Did we just make love in the company car?" she asked, knowing the answer.

Max laughed and nodded his head. "Yes, we did. Haha!"

Eventually, they both put their clothes back on, combed their hair, and tried to make themselves look presentable for their meeting with Lou. Sue giggled all the way into the city.

"I wonder if he's going to notice anything different about us..." Sue pondered aloud.

"Wasn't that great? I felt so...free!" he admitted with a sigh. But she could almost see a sadness in his face—sadness that their "freedom" was over so quickly. Then he turned to her with a grin, "Make sure you don't have a corn stalk in your hair, though." Sue checked her hair, then realized he was just kidding her.

She thought she might be falling in love.

* * * * *

They sat across from Lou and downloaded the case video recording of the man and woman kissing.

"Good job. I'll call his wife and have her come to the office to see the video, hear the conversation, and identify Carla. She'll have what she needs for her attorney."

Maxim and Sue got up from their chairs and headed into the main office area where Kelsey and Monica were working diligently.

"Monica," Max called out, interrupting her computer keying.

She looked up and smiled. "What do you need, Maxim?"

"Keys to the supply room. We need to return the equipment and look at what we might need for the next assignment."

"Sure," Monica said as she opened her desk drawer, picking out a ring of keys, and handing them to Max.

"C'mon, Sue," he beckoned with a nod of his head. He unlocked the room and she followed him inside, closing the door behind them.

They grabbed each other in a frenzy of kisses. There was barely time to breathe. They both knew they couldn't stay in there indefinitely without Monica checking up on them, so they finally parted lips and stared at each other.

"Oh my God," Sue whispered breathlessly. "We're like animals!" They kissed again.

Maxim pulled himself away momentarily and grinned from ear to ear. "And I love every second of it."

He considered their next encounter. They couldn't keep meeting in the supply closet; one of them needed an apartment. "So, you live with your parents?" he asked with a quirky look on his face.

"Yes. For now," Sue responded, understanding the meaning behind the question. "And you live with Monica?"

"Yes. For now. I'm thinking about getting an apartment. I'll let you know if I find one soon."

They kissed again, straightened their clothing, then picked up a few items to look like they were preparing for another case. As they exited the room, Monica, Kelsey, and Lou were all leaning on the desks with their arms folded, facing them.

"Got what you need?" Lou inquired with those same eyes and voice he used to interrogate people.

Sue's face turned beet red.

"Yes, we're all set," Maxim explained, stretching the truth.

"Uh huh," Lou responded, nodding his head. Monica and Kelsey were grinning like Cheshire cats. "Well, get to work. You're on the clock."

"Yes, sir," Sue said meekly. They both scrambled to their desks. Sue and Maxim glanced at each other and smiled. Words weren't necessary.

* * * * *

Three days later Max texted, saying that he found an apartment and he'd be moving in over the weekend. He sent her the address and asked if she'd like to check it out on Saturday.

Silly question.

❧ 40 ❧

Saturday finally arrived and Sue thought about visiting Maxim in his new apartment. Opening his text with his address, she sent him a short note saying that she was on her way.

Sue arrived in about 15 minutes and found a parking spot a few doors away. When she rang the doorbell for Apt. 2 on the second floor, she heard someone racing down the stairs. Maxim opened the door with a wide grin.

"Sue! I'm so glad you came!" he exclaimed with joy. "Come on in!" His dark hair was tousled and his jeans had holes in the knees.

After climbing the rather steep staircase, they entered a large living room with hardwood floors, two windows, and a door that led to an open porch which overlooked the street. Maxim showed her the kitchen, which was small and somewhat rough, but fine for one person. He also had an old-style pantry with plenty of storage space. A modest bathroom with a clawfoot tub and large bedroom were down a small hallway. Maxim was still unpacking, but admitted he'd have to buy some furniture since he only had an old couch and an overstuffed chair.

As they talked, they held onto each other's waist with their hips meeting. Then they kissed, continuing to stand, with neither one wanting to break the embrace. His kisses were gentle and soft. Her thoughts were lost in love. Soon their kisses became more passionate and their hands wandered to each other's body. Maxim led her to the worn but comfy couch where they kissed and touched. He unbuckled and unzipped his jeans, pushing them down and off. She slipped out of hers as well. He found himself on top of her, breathing hard, matching hers, as they made love.

Time went by unnoticed by the pair. Finally, they put themselves back together and Max changed the subject.

Maxim said, "I almost forgot..." He briefly kissed her again.

"What?" she asked, not really caring, as she was more interested in kissing some more.

"I have something for you."

Sue's expression snapped to attention and she looked at him suspiciously. "What do you mean?"

Maxim chuckled. "Look." He pulled out a key from his pocket. "Here's your key to my apartment."

Sue gasped! "Are you serious?"

He put it in her hand. "You're welcome anytime."

She smiled and said, "I love you." Shocked at her own words, she blushed.

Maxim kissed her forehead and said, "I love you, too."

"This happened awfully quick."

"I know. I felt connected to you the first moment I saw you."

She smiled and hugged him. "I felt the same way."

Sue glanced at her fitness watch. "I hate to do this,

Maxim, but I have to get back to work. I have a lead on the case. I'll fill you in as soon as I can." She picked up her purse and headed for the door.

"Okay."

They kissed one more time. He walked her down the stairs to the door. "See you soon."

"Promise?"

"I promise."

They briefly kissed. "Love you. Bye."

"Love you, too. Bye."

Sue walked to her car feeling lighter than air! She stared at the key in her hand. It was almost as thrilling as a ring on her finger. Her life held so much promise now. She had never been so completely happy. It was all-consuming, satisfying, and breathtaking. Sue almost wanted to cry—but for joy.

She figured she would give Maxim some time to get settled and then she'd cook a nice romantic dinner for the two of them. Perhaps buy some candles and place them throughout the apartment. Then, maybe they'd retire to the bedroom and make love the way it was intended. She might even stay the night! Oh, the daydreams and fantasies Sue enjoyed!

In the car, she tuned into a soft-rock radio station and listened to love songs for a change. Up to now, she just couldn't. They were irrelevant and, in fact, sometimes irritating. It just wasn't who she was—then. For the first time, she felt like an adult woman, desiring the pleasures all women enjoy. Her hormones were raging. That made her stop and think about birth control. She made an appointment with the family doctor.

41

Mary Collins walked into Detective Grant's office in Major Crimes. "Steve, take a look at this report from a recent rape case that Kim DeVries is working on."

"Why do I need to look at it?" he questioned, thinking of his already heavy workload.

"You'll see," she coyly replied.

He looked over the familiar coding, then his eyes went to the results. "Gary Ritter?!"

Mary's eyebrows rose as she smirked. "Looks like we got him on another charge."

"Holy smokes!" Steve couldn't believe it, although it wasn't unusual for a serial rapist to graduate to a killer. "When did this happen?"

"The night before we arrested him. The victim went to the hospital the next morning. DeVries handled the rape kit."

"Get DeVries in here," he ordered. "Oh, and thanks, Mary."

About fifteen minutes later, Kim knocked on Steve's open door frame. "Knock, knock. You wanted to see me?"

"Yeah, Kim. Have a seat." He put the DNA report in front of her. "I know you're working on this. Do you know who Gary Ritter is?"

"I just realized you already have him in custody on those murders."

"What can you tell me about the rape?"

Kim shook her head. "The vic has no memory of the guy who did this to her."

Steve rubbed his chin, trying to think. "Let's show her a photo line-up."

* * * * *

A few hours later, Kim DeVries went to the apartment where Katie was staying. Kim, Katie, and Katie's friend Julie sat at the kitchen table.

Julie took Katie's hand and said in a soothing voice, "It's going to be okay. I'm right here."

Kim laid out six 8x10-inch photos on the table. Gary Ritter was No. 5.

"No rush. Look them over carefully. If you see the man who did this to you, write your initials next to his photo."

Katie looked at No. 1, then 2. She stopped a moment to carefully pick up No. 3. She shook her head and put the photo back down. She also examined Numbers 4, 5, and 6. "I don't think it's any of these guys. I know I didn't see any of them at the bar. Sorry."

"Don't be sorry. We'll keep looking," Kim said assuredly. She thanked both of the women and left, feeling a bit confused and disheartened.

When she got back to Major Crimes, she looked at the photos herself. The one that Katie stopped to look at was a dark-haired man who had no resemblance to Gary Ritter. She obviously had no idea who the rapist was. Kim thought it was sad and unfortunate, but perhaps a jury would still find him guilty based on the DNA.

She reported the line-up results to Steve. He was a bit disappointed, too, but felt confident they had the right guy.

42

Everything seemed to happen at once.

First, Sue's dad, Jerry, finished his cancer treatments and had to meet with the oncologist. Sue promised to go with him.

Then the DNA results were due on the black knitted ski mask found near Dan Gilson's house where the mysterious box had been stolen.

Most recently, she and Maxim fell in love.

And now, Carrie sent a brief but urgent text, saying "Come." Sue responded, but there was no reply, and that made Sue very nervous and frightened. She wondered what was going on. There was no telling what Jared might do, and there was also the baby to think about!

She still had a little over two hours before her dad's appointment, so Sue got in her car and sped over to Carrie's. Luckily, it was just a five-minute drive.

Jared's new SUV was nowhere in sight, nor was his old truck. Had he been there and left? She had to know for certain.

Bringing her pistol with her, she found Carrie's front door was open. Protocol was to call 911 and have them clear the house before she entered, but Sue was concerned that there wasn't enough time and Carrie's life, or Justin's life, may be in danger. She drew her handgun, holding it in front of her, ready to fire if necessary.

With her right foot, she gently kicked the bottom of the door so that it swung open all the way while she stayed out of the line of fire. She listened for any movement or distressed or muffled cries. There were none. She glanced around the living room and did not see Carrie or anyone else. There were baby toys scattered, but no sign of little Justin.

Silently entering the house, Sue scanned the first room looking down the barrel of her gun. The tension was indescribable, knowing that an armed man might be around any corner. Fear gripped her until her stomach was in knots and she had to tell herself to breathe. But not too loudly! Not to give herself away. Just enough to stay alive.

Then she headed for the kitchen. Placing her back against the wall, Sue peeked around the doorway into the next room. No one was there. She let out a small sigh. Next, Sue went into the kitchen and looked for any clues or signs of a struggle. There were none. She was relieved to see that all the knives were accounted for in the block on the counter.

Following her procedures, Sue checked every room in the house in the same manner. Carrie and Justin were clearly gone. And there was no trace of her ex, Jared, either.

It took precious time to go through the house, and Sue had to decide what to do next. Since it was possible that Jared took them to his house, Sue decided to head there. If his white SUV was in the driveway, she would call 911 and have the police meet her there. If it wasn't in the driveway, then she would have to come up with another idea. With a heavy foot on the gas, Sue raced to Jared's house.

The vehicle wasn't there.

Sue sat at the curb with her engine idling, thinking about where Jared might go. She didn't know enough about him to make a guess. She decided to take a quick look around the outside of Jared's house.

Just as carefully as she cleared Carrie's house, she also took every precaution going around Jared's property with her gun. The gate to the fence was unlocked, but the yard and shed provided no clues. Sue went to the garage and peered into a side window. There was a boat on a trailer inside, but nothing else of interest. She tried the doorknob on his front door. Locked. She checked for unlocked windows or back door. They were all secure. But as she peered in Jared's kitchen window, there was the stolen wooden box, sitting on his table.

"What the hell?" Sue said aloud. She wondered, *"Why does HE have the box, unless...?"* She felt a chill go down her spine.

Suddenly, she received another text from Carrie. Sue's heart was racing as she read the words, "sos canal." But *where* on the canal? Then Sue remembered the GPS unit she placed under Jared's car. "Why didn't I think of this before?" With her hands shaking, she opened the app to locate his vehicle. It was at the kayak and canoe dock on the canal in a housing tract in Brighton!

It was no longer a situation to deal with herself. She called Chris' direct number on her hands-free phone.

Chris answered, "Sue! What's up?"

"Chris, the murderer has my friend Carrie! I'm going to the canoe dock," she cried.

Stunned, the first words he said were, "What murderer? Which dock?" then realized Sue had hung up. Trusting that Sue knew what she was talking about, he texted her, "On it." The two docks were fairly close to each other. He headed for the first canoe dock with lights and sirens going, hoping it was the right one.

Meanwhile, Sue raced toward the canal dock that was built on the edge of the housing tract. There, she saw the parked, white SUV in the private parking lot. Following her training, Sue exited her vehicle and approached it stealthily, finding it empty. Running to the canal, she looked up and down the waterway. There, about 100 feet offshore, was a blue canoe with two people struggling in the water. At first glance it appeared that they were just holding onto the canoe as best they could. But then Sue realized it was Jared and Carrie and he was trying to loosen her grip.

"Carrie!" Sue shouted.

"Help me!" Carrie cried.

Sue pulled out her phone and called Chris using "redial." She screamed, "I'm jumping in!" then dropped the phone into the dirt.

Shedding her shoes, Sue jumped from the dock into the cold water of the canal, thankful that she had learned how to swim as a youngster and her recent sessions at the gym strengthened her arm muscles as well as her core. Still, the cold water quickly left her breathless. As she swam out to the canoe, she could hear Carrie's screams and gasps for air as Jared pushed her head under the water time and time again.

Sue listened for police sirens but heard nothing as yet. She hoped Chris would find them soon!

Sue made it to the canoe. Jared gave her a menacing look as he continued to push Carrie's head down. Carrie was losing her battle to get enough air. Rather than fight with Jared, Sue pulled Carrie away from him and held her head above water.

Jared, realizing it was two against one, swam toward ashore with the long, strong strokes of an Olympic swimmer. He got to the dock first.

Sue swam sidestroke with Carrie's head locked in her elbow. Once at the dock, Sue was able to place Carrie's arms around a piling while Sue pulled herself out of the water.

"Sue," Carrie gasped, "He's got my gun!" Sue paused for a second to think about this, then turned to run after Jared, who was racing toward his SUV. Both were soaked to the skin, with clothes weighing them down.

He turned his head and realized Sue was right behind him. Jared had no idea who this crazy woman was and why she got involved.

Sue grabbed his arm and spun him around, so that he was now facing her. Those boxing lessons paid off as she punched him with her right and left fists in his solar plexus, as hard as she could.

He felt his breath knocked out of him.

Keeping her body straight, her elbows by her waist, fists toward her, and weight on her left foot, Sue twisted to give Jared a left hook to his face. Stepping forward on her right foot, she gave him a powerful right uppercut to the bottom of his jaw. Jared fell on his back—down and dazed, but not totally out.

Suddenly, she heard Carrie scream to her, "Help me! I can't hold on anymore!"

Making a split decision, Sue headed for the dock, where Carrie was losing her grip on the piling. She pulled her onto the dock, where she collapsed.

Sue turned back toward Jared and watched him pull out of the parking lot with no concern for other vehicles, squealing his tires, and stepping on the gas.

Then he was gone.

Going back to Carrie, she checked to make sure she was okay. She was exhausted but otherwise well enough to stand. Arm in arm, they walked toward Sue's SUV.

A minute later, Chris arrived at the dock, along with other police vehicles and an ambulance. Carrie was taken to the ambulance to be evaluated. Sue dismissed the EMTs who attempted to check her out, and, instead, ran to Chris.

In a panic-stricken voice, Sue cried out, "He tried to kill Carrie! He drove away. White SUV. New."

"What's his name?" Chris asked.

"Jared. Jared Poole."

"We're on it!" Chris responded, then talked into his radio. "APB. Late model, white SUV belonging to Jared Poole. He's probably headed south on 390. Suspicion of attempted murder."

"He's armed!" Sue added.

Chris continued speaking into the radio, "Suspect is armed and dangerous." The police dispatcher repeated the information back to him and to the other officers in pursuit.

"Sue, are you alright?" Chris asked with concern, now that the situation was in the hands of other units.

"I'm good. Thank you for getting here so quickly."

He put his arm around her. "Shhh, it's all over and your friend is safe."

Sue nodded in agreement as her teeth chattered.

"Did sh..she say anything about her baby? Justin wasn't at the house."

Concerned, Chris went to the ambulance and asked Carrie about Justin, then returned to Sue.

"He's at his grandmother's."

Sue breathed a sigh of relief.

An EMT came over to her and gave her a blanket to wrap around her soaked clothes.

As she warmed her body, she asked Chris, "I promised my dad I'd take him to his doctor's appointment this afternoon. Any chance I could go home and check in with you in a couple of hours?"

"I'm sure the detectives have plenty of interviewing before thcy see you." He stepped aside and used his radio.

"Sue, go ahead and take care of your dad. Do you want me to take you home?"

"No, that's okay. I can drive myself. Let me know if you catch that S.O.B." She handed the blanket to Chris and headed for her SUV.

* * * * *

On the 390-South Expressway, Jared, wet from his unexpected swim, was speeding toward Pennsylvania. From there, he would go southwest to the Appalachian Mountains. He had an old school buddy who ran a furniture outlet in a rural area and was hoping he'd let him stay a few nights, if he could just get there! It would give him time to plan where to go next.

His biggest regret was that his plan did not work. Carrie still had Justin and he did not. He may never see Justin again! That was a frightening thought. He became emotional and angry all over again. He thought, *"Why did that woman have to show up when she did? I was so close to fulfilling my plan!"* He pounded his steering wheel.

As he sped down the expressway, the tension built for Jared as he looked in his rear-view mirror. Lights of a police car flashed behind him! "Shit!" he yelled. He stepped on the accelerator—75, 80, 90, 100 miles per hour. He was weaving in and out of traffic, squeezing between cars, riding on the right shoulder spewing cinders and dirt into the air, and cutting off tractor trailers, playing a dangerous game of highway cat and mouse with the police.

The police received several 911 calls from truckers and frantic motorists. They knew it was Jared and they also knew they had to end this chase. He would be pursued until caught due to the seriousness of his crime. They radioed to get the help of State Troopers.

Just as he passed the Conesus exit, Jared realized that a trooper's car was closing the gap on him. He increased his speed. So did the trooper.

Jared opened his window, and with his right hand, he fired a shot from his gun without aiming. The bullet whizzed by the vehicle behind him. Jared fired a second shot. This time it hit the trooper's front fender.

The trooper called into his radio, "Shots fired! Shots fired!" Knowing this was an extremely dangerous situation, he had to stay focused and in control or it may not end well. Finally, the expressway was free of other vehicles.

The trooper tried to get alongside of Jared's SUV but Jared swerved to avoid him.

Gaining back proximity to the white SUV, the trooper did a pit maneuver, tapping the back corner of Jared's vehicle. It skidded sideways, leaving swerving tread marks as the fleeing man tried to get the vehicle under control. Jared was now facing the wrong way down the expressway. Once again, he stepped on the gas, forcing southbound cars in the far-left lane to move over or drive off the road. Even though his primary objective was to head south, he was driving north again. He had to turn around somehow. He found a "no-U-Turn" area, and did a complete 180, so that he could head south—once again at speeds exceeding 95 miles an hour.

A second state trooper caught up to him and attempted a second pit maneuver. Jared tried to correct, but, at 100 miles per hour, it was useless. The SUV flipped into the sky, side over side. When it landed on the road, the metal against the asphalt caused a flash of sparks to fly as it skidded for 100 feet until it hit the soft shoulder, which led to the SUV flipping over and over once again, until it finally stopped on its side on the grass.

The trooper and other pursuing cars pulled up *en masse*, with their guns pointed at the offending driver.

Jared had hit his head on the side window and lost consciousness momentarily. After regaining his senses, he realized there was no place to go. Two police officers pulled him out of his wrecked vehicle. They turned him over and handcuffed him, face down in the grass. Then they grabbed him by his arms and stood him up, leading him to the back of a cruiser where he sat until a medical unit arrived to determine the extent of his injuries.

"What happened?" Jared kept asking over and over. He didn't seem to have any memory of the accident, so he was checked for a concussion and sent to the ER.

Jared was charged with two counts of attempted murder, plus evading, and numerous traffic violations. Other charges were pending and there was much more investigating to do.

43

"What the devil?" Sue's mom exclaimed as Sue walked through the door, her hair still wet and leaving small drips on the floor. "Did you go swimming?"

"You could say that. I'll just take a quick shower and I'll be ready to take Dad to the doctor in a few minutes."

The hot, steamy water felt so good, she didn't want the shower to end.

It was over! Her first real case—Carrie's case—was solved! There were all kinds of questions that still needed to be answered, though. *"In due time,"* she thought.

Refreshed, Sue helped her dad into the car and headed for the oncologist's office, not far from the canal where she had just pulled her friend to safety. She imagined that the police were still on scene.

Jerry saw that she was preoccupied. He asked, "A lot on your mind?"

She snapped out of her trance-like state, looked briefly at her dad, and smiled. "I did have a busy day, but now I'm here for you."

They arrived at the doctor's office building and went inside the waiting room until they were called. After Jerry's vital signs were taken by a technician, they had another few minutes before the doctor showed up.

"So, Dad, how are you feeling today?"

"Pretty good. Glad those treatments are over. Now I hope to get my sense of taste and smell back."

"It might take a month or two, but you'll be fine."

Doctor Reiser knocked on the door then entered. "Hello, Jerry. How are you doing?"

"You tell me, Doc."

"At least he still has a sense of humor," Sue thought.

"Let's take a look at your test results." He paused. "Hmm, things are looking good!" He smiled and Jerry and Sue smiled, too. It had been a long road.

Dr. Reiser checked his lungs and heart, asked him a number of questions, and a short time later, they were back outside.

Sue said, "I think we need to celebrate."

"Haha! I need to feel a little stronger, then I'll think about celebrating."

"How about if I give you a nice neck massage?"

"That sounds great."

"I love you, Dad."

"I love you, too."

Sue began her day feeling overwhelmed but had no idea just how crazy the day would get. She recalled Lou's words, "Expect the unexpected."

Briefly thinking about Maxim, Sue intended to give him a call later, but then she drifted off to sleep on the living room couch for an hour, exhausted from the already busy day. When she awoke, she knew she needed to speak to Detective Grant as soon as possible. Maxim would have to wait.

❧ 44 ❧

June had slipped away, and summer was in full swing, with temperatures nearing 90 degrees. The past few summers were hotter than normal and it looked like this year would be no exception.

Sue faced a long day of meetings with the police detectives. She took the thumb drive in a plastic bag to explain about the secret compartment in the wooden box, which they would seize from Jared's house. She felt relieved that Jared was no longer a threat to her friend Carrie, baby Justin, and Carrie's mother Judy.

The big mystery for Sue was Jared's involvement with the box and the murder of Emily Rogers. She just couldn't put the pieces together in her head. Sue needed to hear Jared's confession, if there was one. He could, of course, ask for his lawyer.

Detective Steve Grant shook Sue's hand as he welcomed her back to Major Crimes. They were joined by Detective Brian Sills of the Brighton Police Department.

"Jared was released from the hospital and is now in custody, charged with attempted murder. He went through all the processing, including fingerprinting, photo identification, and DNA testing," Grant said. "Why do you think he's the canal killer, Sue?"

"I can tell you what I know, but there's still a lot I don't know."

"Okay, let's go in the interview room and you can give your statement," Grant said.

"If you can, bring a laptop with a USB port," Sue suggested.

Inside the interrogation room, Sue felt a coldness she hadn't experienced before. This was the room not only for witnesses, but also for persons of interest and suspects. It was almost as if the room were haunted by evil souls, still active and roaming the earth. How many had sat where she sat and confessed to horrendous crimes? It was chilling and made her shudder.

Detective Grant informed Sue that her statement would be video recorded. He voiced the date and time of the interview, as well as a case number.

Sue began with the missing person's case for Emily Rogers and how she found the purse and its contents on the Canalway Trail and linked it to the Walmart in Gates. She also mentioned the surveillance videos in the Walmart parking lot where Emily got out of a dark pickup truck and returned to the same truck. After the truck moved to the back of the lot, it exited the parking lot and headed in the direction of the expressway. That was confirmed by some CCTV cameras along the way. The same pickup truck was seen on cameras at the exit near the canal in Brighton. And later that week, she and Maxim found earbuds which matched those that Emily lifted during that same shopping trip. There appeared to be blood on the wires, so she called 911. The police later located the body in the canal.

So far, the detectives had nothing to add or question, as they had followed the same leads.

Then Sue told them that she and Lou Perlo went back to Emily's house and found the receipt for the wooden box purchased by Dan Gilson. They went to see Dan, who seemingly had a poor memory of Emily, and identified the box. It wasn't until a few days later that they met Tristen and heard his side of the story. He knew nothing about the box.

Sue continued, "The box kept nagging at me. I felt there had to be something important about it. I went back to Dan and asked if I could borrow it. That's when I found this inside the box." She held up the black-and-red thumb drive which had been put into a clean plastic bag and sealed. "You're going to want to open it."

Detective Grant left the room to get a pair of gloves to handle the thumb drive. He returned and put the drive into the port. There was only one folder, called "Trolley." He clicked on it. Sills pulled his chair closer so that he could see the screen. Sue saw their faces as they went through the photos of the unidentified woman.

"It's Sarah Bennington!" Grant cried out.

The shock was felt by everyone in the room, since not even Sue knew who the victim was in those photos.

Once again, Sue went on with her story. "Apparently, only the killer knew those photos were there. Emily was clueless about the contents of the box, as was Dan Gilson. Neither of them had ever opened the box. It remained a secret until my father figured out the trigger to open the box and I examined the files. I had no idea who the girl was or whether or not she survived. I replaced the original thumb drive in the box with an identical one but containing my own photos."

Detective Grant interrupted. "I still don't see the connection to Jared Poole."

"Neither do I," Sue admitted. "But someone stole the box for one reason only: to get that thumb drive out of there before Dan opened it and called the police. That someone was Jared Poole. The box is sitting on his kitchen table. I saw it when I looked through his window."

"What made you suspect Jared?" the detective inquired.

"I didn't!" Sue explained that she was just looking out for her girlfriend Carrie and that Jared was her ex-boyfriend and the father of their child. "I was tracking Jared with a GPS when I got an urgent text from Carrie asking for help. I tracked him to the canoe dock."

"Why a canoe, I wonder?" Sills asked.

Thinking back, Sue recalled Jared's garage. "Oh! Jared has a boat and trailer in his garage. Maybe he didn't have enough time to hook it up to his SUV."

"That will be one of our questions when we interrogate him. We still have one important piece of the puzzle missing. Why didn't we find Jared's DNA at either murder scene?"

45

A 911 call had been received while the detectives were interviewing Sue. A woman said she had information about the Emily Rogers murder. When Detective Grant came back to his office, he returned her cell phone call.

"Hello, Christy? We got your call. Do you think you could come down to the police station and give us a statement?"

"Yeah. It'll take me about 30 minutes. I'll see you then." They ended the call.

Sills offered up his opinion, "I think we should wait until we hear what she has to say before we question this Jared character."

"I agree. She might have something that either fingers him or someone else," Grant answered.

And so, they waited.

Grant and Sills allowed Sue to sit in another room where a monitor was set up to watch Christy's questioning. Sue was joined by a few other detectives who were interested in the case.

Shortly after her arrival, a woman, identified as Christy Duggins, was shown into the interview room. Grant observed her appearance and demeanor on the monitor. Her bleached blonde hair was rather wild, and she showed off a deep tan next to her stretchy white tube top and black shorts. She seemed quite agitated.

The detectives entered the room and introduced themselves. She smiled nervously.

"Hi. Can I have a smoke?"

"This shouldn't take too long, Christy. What exactly do you know about the murder of Emily Rogers?"

"I saw it."

They were stunned. "Why don't you start at the beginning?" Grant suggested.

She explained that she and a guy named Rich had been dating for a couple of months but a girlfriend of hers saw another girl in his truck.

Grant interrupted her. "Whoa. Rich who?"

"Rich Landers!" she said, exasperated, as if they should already know.

Grant and Sills looked at each other. They both were thinking, *"Shit! We may have the wrong guy in custody,"* but they kept listening.

"How did you meet Rich?" Sills asked.

"On Tinder. He looks older in person."

"Go on. What happened the day of the murder?

"Well, my girl Tonya spotted Rich's truck in the Walmart parking lot in Gates with some other bitch. Tonya called me right away. I drove over there and saw that the bitch must have been giving him a blow job because her blue head suddenly popped up in the front seat of his truck. When Rich pulled out of the lot, I followed them. I didn't know where the hell he was going 'cause he got on the expressway and got off at Town Line Road, then doubled back on Clinton. They pulled into the parking lot by the canal and got out. I drove by the lot and turned around. When I got back to the parking lot, they already were out of the truck and on the trail."

Realizing that she knew facts not widely known to the public, Grant felt she was telling the truth. He asked, "So what did you do?"

"I followed them! What the hell? I wanted to give him a piece of my mind for cheating on me and tell that bitch she was seeing a two-timing bastard!"

"Did you? Give him a piece of your mind, that is."

"No," she said distractedly. "Are you sure I can't have a smoke?" There was no response.

"Why didn't you?" Grant pressed on.

"I sure could use that cigarette." Christy was nervously playing with her hair.

"Okay," Grant said, surrendering to her addiction. Sills went out and brought back an ashtray, some cigarettes and a lighter into the room. She lit one up and took a long draw in, then blew the smoke out the side of her mouth. It seemed to relax her.

"Well, they were ahead of me. Once, Rich looked back and I had to duck behind a bush."

"What were they doing?"

"Just walking. He had his arm around her. She was listening to music, I think."

"And then?"

"He strangled the girl! I saw the whole thing! I was afraid he'd kill me, too, so when he had his back to me, I ran back to my car. I didn't see no more." She took another draw on her cigarette and blew the smoke away from Grant's face.

Sills stood up. "Steve, let's look him up." They both left the room and went to the computer.

Sue came out of the side room. "Detective Grant! There were texts to a Rich on Emily's phone!"

"Got it," he replied, accepting her information. He sat at his computer and typed in Rich's name into the system. Nothing came up. He widened the search but still nothing. He sat back in his chair.

Mary Collins came by his desk and saw that he looked frustrated. "What's up?" she asked.

"Can't find a guy. There's nothing on him. Not sure what to do next."

She cocked her head to the side. "Why not show her a picture of that Jared guy you have in the other room. See if she knows him."

"Mary, I was thinking the same thing! Maybe we aren't looking for the wrong suspect!" He printed out a photo of Jared and five other similar-looking men around 30 years old. He took the sheet into Christy.

"Okay, Christy, I've got six photos of men on this sheet. Perhaps none of them are the guy we're looking for, but if you recognize someone, circle his picture and add your initials." He put a pen on the table.

He flipped the sheet over. She looked through the photos, and yelled, "That's him! Number 5!"

"Who is that?"

"Rich Landers!" She circled his photo with the pen and initialed it.

"Thank you, Christy. You've been a big help." Detective Grant stood and showed her the door. She took the cigarettes with her as she left.

Before Grant went into the interrogation room to speak to Jared, he stopped to see Sue Gainer.

"Sue, we got a positive id."

She looked confused. "What do you mean?"

"Jared is Rich."

"What? How can that be? I don't understand."

"We'll see what happens in his interview."

He was about to interrogate Jared when Carrie arrived at the station. She was ushered in to see Detective Grant, who was already standing in the doorway.

"I've come to make my statement against Jared," she said with determination.

"Let's do it," Grant proposed. "Follow me." He looked back at Sue with a smile—one of those smiles that reveals satisfaction and enlightenment. Or perhaps the cat was about to be let out of the proverbial bag.

❧ 46 ❧

In the interview room, Detective Grant began the recording.

"Carrie, I hope you're doing okay," Grant said sincerely.

"I'm just grateful Sue and the police showed up when they did." Carrie shivered thinking about the danger she had been in.

"So, tell me what happened today."

"Jared wanted to see my son...uh, our son, but he doesn't have custody and I really don't want him around. I filed an order of protection, but that didn't stop him."

"When did you file that?"

"A week ago."

"Okay." Grant made a note. "Go on."

"I took the baby—Justin—to my mom's this morning. When Jared showed up at my house, I texted Sue and asked her to come. Jared said he was going to go to Mom's house and see Justin. I warned him, saying, 'You'd better not. You stay away from my baby and my mother!' He laughed and headed toward his new car that had a canoe on top, which I thought was odd. I grabbed his arm. When he turned around, he had this evil look on his face that I had never seen before," she told him. "It scared me."

"What kind of car does he have?"

"It's a white SUV. It's new. Before that, he had a black pickup."

Inside the monitor room, Sue jumped up. "Black pickup? Why didn't I put two and two together?" No one else seemed to key in on that information. "I need to talk to Detective Grant!"

Detective Sills told Sue that she'd have to wait. She sat back down on the edge of her seat.

In the interview room, Grant continued, "So, what did he do then, Carrie?"

"He grabbed my arm and said, 'I guess we'll go together then!' He pulled me to his car and made me get in. I was afraid that if I didn't go, he might try to take Justin or hurt my mom."

"You never thought to call 911?"

"Oh. Guess not," she confessed. "I was just so worried about my baby!"

"Then what happened?"

"When he took off, he didn't drive to my mom's. He went to the canal. I asked, 'What are we doing here?'"

"He said, 'We're going for a paddle.' I said, 'A canoe ride?' I didn't like the sound of it."

"But you got in?"

"I did, but I texted an SOS to Sue. Before I knew it, Jared was rocking the canoe and I fell in. So did he. Then he tried to push my head down, and...." Carrie burst into tears. She grabbed a couple of tissues from her purse and wiped her nose. "He tried to kill me!"

"Carrie, I need to ask you a question. Have you ever heard of Rich Landers?"

She looked confused. "No." She shook her head. Her eyes were teary and red.

"How about Gary Ritter?"

"Gary Ritter? I know that name. Not that I know him, but it rings a bell." She thought for a moment. "Wait! I got it!"

"Tell me about him."

"He donated his bone marrow to Jared and saved his life!"

Detective Grant felt goosebumps all over his body. "Bone marrow?" He paused. "I'll be right back." He stood up and left the room.

He went to see Mary Collins at her desk. "Mary, have you ever heard of anyone having a bone marrow transplant and getting someone else's DNA?"

"Yes, as a matter of fact. It was in the news a few months back. The person who gets the bone marrow may not only take on the donor's DNA, but sometimes the DNA change alters looks and mannerisms, too."[*]

"So, you're saying that it's possible for two people to have the same DNA?"

"Yes. They become a 'genetic chimera.'"

"What's that?"

"I think it's when you have your DNA in your cells and also your bone-marrow donor's DNA in your blood. If I remember right, the donor's DNA is in the cells that line the mouth, so a buccal swab may not be considered as evidence in a court of law."

That information stunned him. He considered it for a minute or two, then went to see his colleagues.

He gave them the rundown of what Mary had told him. Sue listened intently.

---

[*] Roger Schlueter, Belleville News-Democrat, MedicalXpress, January 19, 2018, Home/Health, https://medicalxpress.com/news/2018-01-bone-marrow-transplant-dna.html

"I think we had this case all wrong!" he declared, then went on to explain.

Sue spoke up. "Lieutenant! Jared used to drive a black pickup truck! That's the vehicle that was spotted in the Walmart parking lot! Maybe he traded it in!"

Grant turned to his detectives. "Get the make and model and VIN. See where he bought it. Maybe his trade-in is still there."

Sue popped up, "I'd like to go."

"Sure. Ride with Detective Pratt." Molly Pratt was a no-nonsense female detective with flaming red hair, who didn't mess around. She was known for her keen eye and strict discipline.

"Thanks!" Sue went with her.

After checking her computer, Detective Pratt was confident that she knew where the SUV was purchased.

"Let's go!"

Sue followed her out to an unmarked police car. It was a 15-minute drive to the dealership on the west side of town. They exited their car and went directly to the main office.

"I'm Detective Pratt with the Rochester Police Department," she announced to the well dressed, older man sitting at a desk, wearing a tan suit and subdued-color tie. "We are working a homicide and we need some information about a black pickup truck that might have been traded-in recently."

"Certainly," agreed the man, who identified himself as the owner of the dealership.

"The person of interest may have purchased a white SUV. I have the VIN." She recited the number.

He looked it up. "Yes, we sold that SUV to a Jared Poole. And yes, he traded in a pickup truck. We sent it directly to the auction house in Victor. Here's the VIN of the truck."

"Did you take a picture of it?" Pratt asked.

"No, but the auction house would have. Here's their card with their number." He handed her a business card.

"Thanks. Have a good day."

Molly and Sue got back in the car and entered the expressway, heading for the town of Victor on the southeast side of the city.

They went into the main office of the auction business. A casually dressed man offered to help.

"Do you still have a black pickup truck with the VIN...?" Molly read it off.

After tapping the number into his computer, he said, "Sure do! Has a little damage but it's a good vehicle."

"Has it been detailed?"

"Um, no. Good thing you found it today. Tomorrow it was going to auction. There's some interest."

"We'd like to take a look at it."

The three of them walked out into the lot. The sun was beating down on them as they looked around.

Sue spotted it, "There it is! The one with the front-end damage!"

"Sue, don't touch it," Molly warned. "We'll have enough work to sort out fingerprints as it is."

They both peered inside. Pratt used her torch to shine into the truck's interior.

"Look!" Sue shouted, pointing to the front passenger seat. "Blue hair!"

Pratt took control. "Sir, the Rochester Police Department is going to impound this vehicle in connection with a homicide. No one is to touch this truck."

"Yes, Ma'am." He stuffed his hands inside of his pants pockets while he thought about the money he'd lose.

She made a call on her cell. Molly and Sue waited until a patrol car showed up to supervise the loading of the vehicle onto a flatbed truck, then drove back to Major Crimes, anxious to learn of any new details in the case.

༄ 47 ༄

Jared was led into Interview Room #1 in a white, disposable jail onesie, paper slippers, and handcuffs, where he sat on the same chair that Sue had used a few hours prior. Grant and Sills walked in with the laptop and sat across from him, handing him a can of pop.

"Mr. Poole, I'm Detective Grant and this is Detective Sills." He paused and looked at Jared to determine where to start.

"So, why don't you tell us what happened yesterday?"

There was no response, as Jared took a few gulps of the soda.

Grant tried again. "We need to hear your side of the story, Jared. This is your one chance to tell us."

"I don't remember much. My head..."

Understanding that Mr. Poole suffered a slight concussion but had been released from the hospital, Detective Grant decided to approach the questioning in a different way.

"Do you have a baby son?"

Jared's eyes lit up. "I do. He's all I ever wanted, but the judge said I can't have custody or shared custody."

"Why is that?"

"Carrie. His mom. She keeps fighting it."

"How do you feel about that?"

"Mad as hell. She won't even let me see him." Grant thought that he was going to start crying.

"What happened to refuse that right to you?"

Looking perplexed, Jared shook his head. "Probably because I started seeing another girl." Then he quickly pointed out, "It didn't last. I went back to Carrie."

"Did you have a fight about it with Carrie?"

"We are always fighting," Jared admitted.

"Did you ever strike her?"

Remembering that day long ago was easier than remembering the day before. "I accidentally hit her when I was swinging my arms."

"We know those things happen," the detective slyly confided.

"Yeah, she was just being a bitch about it."

"Did Carrie throw you out?"

He nodded his response.

"How did you feel about that?"

"In a way, I was glad. She wanted me to do all the housework while she took care of Justin. It wasn't going to happen, y'know? That's her job! At least when I was on my own, I did what I wanted."

"Did you date?"

"Yeah, sure!"

"Who did you date?"

"Who?" Jared thought about his response. The detective didn't want to give him time to contrive a story.

"What was her name?"

"Well, there were a few girls. There was Christy, and um..." Jared did not provide any other names.

"Jared, maybe these pictures will refresh your memory." Placing social media pictures of both Sarah and Emily on the table, Grant asked, "Do these girls look familiar?"

After glancing at both pictures, Jared looked away.

"Mr. Poole. We already know what happened; we just need you to tell us."

Perhaps thirty seconds went by with no reply from the suspect. Anxious, Jared's right leg began to make repetitive movements under the table as he twisted his hands.

"Okay, Jared. Let's go back to Carrie. Do you recall what happened yesterday at the canal?

"Our canoe tipped over," Jared offered as his explanation. He appeared to be bored.

"How did it tip over?"

"Carrie stood up." He held his hands out in exasperation.

"Were you arguing?"

Giving a snarky reply, Jared said, "She wanted to go swimming. Ha."

"Did you want to swim with her?"

"No..." He shook his head and looked down at the table. "...but the canoe tipped and I ended up in the drink."

Sills asked, "Why didn't you use your motorboat?"

Jared, surprised that the detective knew about his boat, looked up. "My new SUV couldn't pull the boat with the trailer. I don't know what I was thinking when I bought the damn thing. Is my car totaled? I don't remember what happened."

It was apparent that Jared's short-term memory had been affected by the accident and resulting concussion. "I'm afraid so." Then Grant went back to his line of questioning. "But you had a canoe?"

"Yeah. I had to tie it to the rack on the top of the car."

"Why don't you walk us through the whole day. You got up in the morning—when?"

"I hadn't slept. Nothing was going right." He didn't want to tell them about the thumb drive, but that's what he was referring to.

"Go on."

Jared sat in silence, debating whether he should ask for a lawyer or not.

Another detective entered the room and informed Detective Grant, "The gun that was recovered from the SUV? It was stolen. Used in a gas station robbery around Christmas."

Grant looked at Jared, "Where did you get the gun?"

"It's not my gun! It's Carrie's. Ask her!"

"So, you're saying that it wasn't in your possession when you were arrested?"

"It's not my gun." Jared appeared to shut down.

Grant sat back in his chair. He needed Jared to talk. If he asked for a lawyer, it would be all over and the D.A. would have to prove his guilt, not just about the attempted murder but also, possibly, about the murder of two young women. He had to keep the conversation going. He decided to take a different approach.

"How long did you know Emily?"

Jared looked stunned. "Emily?" He nervously shifted in his chair. "I don't know any Emily."

"What about Sarah?"

Jared looked at the lieutenant without emotion, but Grant noticed beads of perspiration on his forehead.

"Did you have a sexual relationship with Sarah and Emily?"

"I don't know what you're talking about."

"Were you going to kill Carrie, too?"

"I told you. The canoe tipped over!" His voice raised.

"Okay, the canoe tipped. When was the last time you saw your son?"

That question struck a chord with Jared. His face turned red and he started grinding his teeth.

"When I went to have it out with Carrie."

"And you're still angry."

"You're damn right I'm angry. He's my flesh and blood!"

"And bone?"

Jared looked a bit confused. "Yeah, and bone. Whatever."

"So, tell me about your bone marrow transplant," Grant baited.

"What about it? I had leukemia and needed a transplant."

"Do you know who donated their bone marrow?"

"Let's see... Oh, it was a guy named Ritter. I never met him, though. Don't even know what he looks like."

"You were never curious?"

"Not really."

"Why is it that I think you're lying about everything, Jared?" There was no response. Steve looked upon a man filled with guilt, just staring at the floor, clearly trying to come up with a believable story.

"Let's go back to Sarah Bennington," Grant continued. "What was it about her that you didn't like? Did she argue with you?"

Jared was getting frustrated. He didn't want to spill his guts about Carrie, or Sarah, or Emily, or anyone else! But obviously this cop had done his homework. He had connected all the dots. Was there anything he didn't already know? Jared knew his own lies were getting him deeper in shit, and he couldn't come up with alibis for all of them. He hadn't thought things through. He needed time! Time to think! And this cop wasn't giving him that time. It was like being surrounded by a firing squad. Every cop had it in for him. He should've done Carrie in at the house and not the canal where he left the bodies of Emily and Sarah. He was mad at himself for being so stupid. He thought the water would erase any evidence and cleanse him of the evil he had done. But the bodies rose from the water and revealed his black soul.

He shook off the thoughts going through his brain and opened his cold, dark eyes, staring at the detective.

"Jared, this is your last chance to tell your side of the story. Detective Sills and I are going to walk out, and you will have to convince twelve members of a jury of your innocence. Don't forget—we have evidence. We have surveillance, DNA, and witness testimony. We know you did these crimes, Jared."

His eyes closed in obvious turmoil. They had him nailed to the wall. "Okay, I'll tell you. I'll tell you everything."

Lieutenant Grant let out a silent sigh. "I'm listening..."

"When I was sick, Carrie was by my side and fell in love with me. Then she got pregnant and gained maybe 40 pounds. It was repulsive. She said she was eating for two, but all I could see was the way she fed her face. She obviously didn't care about me anymore. So I went out and met some girls. Pretty girls. Thin girls. Girls who paid attention to me and flirted with me. I liked the way they made me feel."

He smiled, thinking back to that time.

Grant asked, "Did you have a sexual relationship with any of them?"

"Ha! All of them! They loved it. Then Justin was born and things changed. Carrie kicked me out of the house."

"What caused that? Your infidelity?"

"That, and one of the girls I met accused me of rape."

"But it was just rough sex, right?" Grant baited once again.

"Yeah. She wanted it. She liked it one minute then didn't the next. That's not right. When you're in, you're in. You can't stop when the other person is...well, you know...about to come."

"What did Carrie do to you?"

"I knew Carrie bought a gun because she threatened me with it. So, one night I took that weapon out of her bedroom side table and put it in my car. She didn't even miss it!"

"How did you get in?"

"I still had a key. I thought about using the gun on her when she got home, but I didn't want to get caught. Then she changed the freaking locks."

"You tried to get in?"

"Couldn't. So I left. I had to think of another way of getting rid of her and taking Justin."

"Tell me about Sarah," Grant smoothly interjected.

"Sarah? Yeah, I met Sarah online and her body looked smokin' hot. I couldn't wait to screw her, y'know?" Jared snickered. "But when she took my picture to put on social media, it kinda pissed me off. We had an argument."

"Because you were using an alias on Tinder? Under the name Rich Landers?"

Jared was shocked that Grant knew about Tinder. It took him a minute to respond. "Yeah. What if Carrie found out and made more trouble for me? So, I started thinking maybe I could do in Sarah, you know, as a practice run for Carrie."

"Clever," the detective remarked sarcastically.

"The next week, I asked Sarah to go for a boat ride on the canal. She agreed and thought it was 'romantic.' Romance was not what I had in mind, though," he joked.

"But on the boat, we argued about her missing sunglasses. I must have dropped them somewhere. Anyway, the sun went down and she didn't need them."

Jared continued, "When it got dark, I started thinking about Carrie and getting more and more angry and worked up. When I looked at Sarah, I thought I was looking at Carrie. In the dark, *I couldn't tell the difference...*"

"So you took it out on Sarah?"

"It was time for Carrie to die."

"What did you do to Sarah?"

He hesitated. "I hit her."

"How many times?"

"I'm not sure. Then I strangled her until she wasn't breathing or resisting anymore. When I was done, I pushed her out of the boat. She just sank into the dark water."

He didn't admit that he took pictures of Sarah for his own enjoyment and hid them in the carved box that he gave to Emily.

"That's what you wanted to do to Carrie today?"

Jared seemed to snap out of his past and into the present. "Today? Yeah. But I had to take the canoe, dammit! That messed me up. Then she had to tip it! The bitch!"

"What about Emily, Jared?"

"What? Emily?" He looked confused. "Oh. That's another story..."

∾48∾

Flashback to June 6...

I t was an unusually hot, very quiet, early June day, except for chirping birds. Even the canal water was silent, barely showing movement. As "Rich" and Emily walked the canal trail, he checked their surroundings, glancing up and down the path, and toward the nearest overpass.

Rich looked at Emily and thought she was a "cute little thing" with her shiny blue hair, but very naive. And very stupid. Deadly stupid.

She made a big mistake selling his box. He didn't care that she never looked inside the box or opened the file on the drive to see the pictures. None of that mattered. But the guy she sold it to might be smart enough to open the box and call the cops.

Besides, Rich wanted those pictures. They were his souvenirs—photos of a time he wanted to recall over and over in his plan to eventually kill Carrie. He needed to make sure he did everything exactly right the first time so he'd never be caught.

Rich never saw Sarah in those pictures, just Carrie. They were quite satisfying. The phony profile on social media would make things difficult, if not impossible, for police when they tried to track down someone who didn't exist. He didn't think he forgot anything. Smiling, Rich felt it would be the perfect murder.

Once Carrie disappeared, he would get custody of his son. Then he and Justin could do all the father-son things that other men did—boating, fishing, football, and more. And Carrie wouldn't be there to interfere. Justin would be all his.

Before that could happen, though, he had to make sure Emily couldn't talk to police. She was collateral damage in his plan to kill Carrie and a weak link. He had to quiet her and show no mercy.

When Rich was sure no one was looking, he put his arm around Emily. She turned and smiled at him with her sparkling white teeth and blue lipstick, as she still listened to her music. Her eyes revealed her happiness and ease with his company. Rich was a good-looking guy. Yes, a bit older, but mature and very experienced in sex. He made her very happy, indeed.

A few seconds elapsed between her smile and Rich's response. In one swift move, he grabbed both ends of the earbuds, flipped the wire to the front of her neck, and then twisted the wire around her neck from behind. She let out a single terrified gasp. The weight of her phone made it drop onto the asphalt path and she grasped at the wire around her neck with both hands, to no avail. He continued to twist and yank on the wire. It seemed to take forever to him. It was "forever" to her. In her panic, she was kicking and trying to remove his hands, but he held on with all his might. When the kicking finally stopped and she went limp, he let her drop to the ground. He then dragged her body to the edge of the canal and pushed her over the side. It tumbled through the weedy growth, over the jagged rocks and then into the water. There was one loud splash, then nothing except for a few ripples.

Rich picked up her phone, opened her contacts app, deleted his name, shut down the phone, and threw it as far as he could into the water. He grabbed her purse and started walking on the path back to his vehicle. He planned to empty her wallet and throw the purse into the first dumpster he came across, but he suddenly heard voices coming from the parking area. As he quickly tossed the purse into the shrubbery, some loose items fell out.

An older man with a whiskered face and a skinny kid were in the parking lot. They both looked at Rich. Without looking into their eyes, he got into his truck and left the area, driving to a car dealer on the other side of town to pick up his new SUV.

❧ 49 ❧

Detective Steve Grant had just recorded the cold confession of Jared Poole in the murder of both Emily Rogers and Sarah Bennington. He had one more card to play.

"Jared, let's go back to the night that Carrie changed the locks on her doors."

Jared looked up. "Yeah, I remember."

"What did you do afterwards?"

"Afterwards? I dunno. Let me think." He paused to get his story straight. "I went out drinking."

"How did you feel?"

"Angry. Pissed. Wanting to get even."

"Did you take your anger out on someone else?"

Jared thought about it for a few minutes. "There was a girl at the bar. We went to her place and had sex. That's all."

"Did she willingly go with you?"

"Why shouldn't she?"

"Then why can't she remember anything about that night? Did you put a little something in her drink?"

"Just to loosen her up, y'know?"

"What was her name?"

"Um... Not sure."

Grant opened a manila folder.

The detective showed Jared a photo of Katie that Kim DeVries took of her at the hospital, with contusions on her face.

"I want you to look at this photo and tell me if you recognize her."

Jared grimaced. "She didn't look like that at the bar, but yeah, that's her."

"Did you do this to her?" He paused. "Don't deny it, Jared. We have your sperm, your saliva. Your DNA."

"I think I've done enough talking. I want my attorney."

Grant smiled. "That's okay, Jared. We've got everything we need."

❧ 50 ❧

Tristen carefully planned his magic act. He constructed his set with a table, several decks of cards, an easel and poster with the name Tristen the Magician hand painted in large letters, a black curtain, black tablecloth, smoke capsules and bombs to be used at the right moment, and a turntable with a box large enough to hide an adult. He practiced his trick, although Emily never appeared— but he was certain she would in the final act.

Reading up on tricks of famous magicians, one even made an elephant appear. If he could do that, why not a teenage girl? Of course, the magician had an elephant to begin with; Tristen did not have Emily. However, he believed in himself and in his magic and the powers that be.

Tristen had to bring Emily back or he'd have to give up magic forever. That was the deal he made to himself. It would have to work, or he'd be working on cars for the rest of his life. His parents just shook their heads. Why would their now-adult son think he could bring a girl back from the dead? Was he so enamored with the memory of his girlfriend that he became mentally unstable? Why shame himself in front of strangers, family, and friends? They heard the police and a private detective were also going to attend. For what purpose, they weren't sure, but it concerned them. Did they suspect their son of murdering the girl? Or were they prepared to see something gruesome, like her dead body? They had to allow Tristen to go through with this charade to bring him back to reality, so they took a step back and stood by to give him emotional support when it failed. It was what parents do.

The day of Tristen's performance arrived. It was a lovely summer's day without any threat of rain. When Tristen wasn't busy setting everything up, he was pacing and going through the motions of his act. At other moments, he was praying to God and all the saints to bring his Emily back, and to please allow his act to work.

At noon, he was ready. People started arriving and standing in groups, discussing the trick, the magician, and the possible outcome. Sue Gainer, the private investigator, hung around his set, which made him edgy. He didn't want to give his secrets away. The Gates Police patrol car pulled up to the curb and two officers exited but stood to the side so they could watch the comings and goings of the crowd and examine every face. They started their body cameras.

Everyone held up their cell phones ready for photos or videos. The rumble of voices in the audience grew louder and more agitated. Did this magician really believe his dead girlfriend would come back to life? Would they be looking at a dead body? Or just an empty box? Or, worse, was this just a practical joke to get people to show up so he could perform some dumb card tricks?

At 12:30, Tristen put on his magician's attire. It wasn't the typical tall black hat, cape, magic wand, and bouquets of fake flowers and ribbons up his sleeve, but he was prepared to release smoke at the right time so that his trick could not be visible to the audience. He said a last-minute prayer, took a deep breath, and stepped out in front of the crowd forming on his lawn.

There was a smattering of clapping and a few voices cheering him on. A few other voices were jeering. Tristen paid no heed to the non-believers.

"Good afternoon, ladies and gentlemen, boys and girls!" His face looked hopeful, joyful.

"I am Tristen, the Magician, and today you will witness nothing less than a miracle! I will make a woman appear from nothing on this very stage. Yes, ladies and gentlemen, I will make my dear friend Emily Rogers return from the dead and appear in the black box you see before you!"

There was a loud murmuring in the crowd. The eyes of the police were on him as well.

"But first, let me prepare you for the big event." Tristen performed some card tricks where the cards changed before their eyes, and went up in a puff of smoke, disappearing altogether. Then, with a quick hand gesture, the cards were all back in his hand. He spread them out for the audience to see. He smiled, hearing a few gasps and aahs coming from the crowd. Everything was going as planned.

After two more card tricks with audience participation, everyone began to have faith in Tristen and his magic. Yes, here was a true magician. So clever, so quick, so perfect that no one could figure out how he did his sleight of hand. Tristen was feeling the confidence now. He was ready for the big reveal.

"And now—the moment you've all been waiting for!" His heart was beating wildly.

A thundercloud drifted overhead in the once blue sky. It rumbled, threatening rain.

The crowd tightened and moved closer to the small stage. Everyone wanted a close-up view of what was to occur.

"As you can see, there is nothing in this box." He turned it on the turntable, knocked on the back wooden panel, put his hand inside the empty cavity and knocked on all sides, to show that it was just a box, and nothing more. No secret panels, and no entry from the floor. He completely covered the box with a very large black sheet.

There was a crack of thunder. The audience was getting nervous and hoped he'd "step it up."

Sue watched with interest as she stood close by. All eyes were on the box, so no one noticed when she slipped behind Tristen's set. Tristen turned the box slowly one more time. She could hear him speaking to the audience, saying "Let's all say the magic word: 'Abracadabra!'" The crowd echoed it. "I give you...Emily Rogers!!!" He whipped off the sheet and exploded a smoke bomb.

As if planned, thunder roared overhead and lightning flashed, blinding everyone momentarily. There were some screams from a few women in the crowd.

But when the smoke cleared, there was no one standing inside the box.

Tristen's heart dropped. He wondered, *"How could I have screwed this up?!"*

The crowd booed and hissed and made disappointing sounds when there were no photo opportunities. No pictures for social media. No hype. No excitement. None at all. Just what appeared to be an empty box. The crowd started to disperse in all directions as rain began to fall. Everyone looked sad or mad, and now they were all getting wet.

But Tristen, who was shocked at his own failure, looked at the inside of the box a second time. Something looked different.

"Wha...what is that?"

There on the floor of the black box was a silver ring—the one Emily wore on her ring finger. Tristen picked it up. There were also several strands of iridescent blue hair on the ring.

"Oh my God!" he exclaimed as he held his prize. "She was here!!" He fell to his knees and started crying from joy, as rain soaked his hair and hands.

With the roar of the pouring rain, his parents couldn't understand what he was saying. Thinking he was crying from disappointment, they approached with sadness and acceptance. "Come, Son. Let's go inside," his dad said. "We shouldn't be outside in a thunderstorm." His dad put an arm around Tristen but he shook it off.

"Dad, look! She was here! Here's her ring and her hair!"

Mr. Phillips was stunned, especially when he saw the hair. "How the hell...?" He looked at his son and wondered what dark magic he had concocted to produce the ring off the finger of a dead girl.

One of the police officers wanted to see the ring, as well. Sue stepped in front of the officer and shook her head. She said in a low voice, "Officer, I'm Sue Gainer. I work for Lou Perlo. About the ring. I slipped it in the box. The ring is from Emily's mother. Here's my card if you want to check it out." He looked at the card, then looked at Sue. "Okay. Thanks. Good luck with the kid." He and the other officer headed for their police cruisers.

Now soaked by the sudden rainstorm, Sue walked over to Tristen, who was still beaming with joy. He showed her the ring and strands of blue hair. She thought, *"How weird! Where did the hair come from? I didn't put it in the box!"*

She could offer no explanation as she stared at it.

It must have been magic!

❦ 51 ❦

When Sue walked into the office, everyone was speaking in a whisper and then stopped suddenly with all eyes on her, as though they didn't want her to hear something. She felt a little hurt by it. *"What's this all about?"* she wondered. *"Have I done something wrong? Am I going to be let go?"* A moment of panic set in. *"Maybe I didn't work out!"* She also thought it might have something to do with her relationship with Maxim. *"How much do they know?"*

She looked at each one of them suspiciously as she walked to her desk in the corner of the office. Lou approached her.

"Sue, can you spare a moment to meet with us?"

She swallowed and said, "Sure." She stood up and walked over to Monica's and Kelsey's desks, which were next to each other. Lou, Kelsey, and Monica stood around Sue.

Lou began. "Sue. It's been a pleasure working with you…"

"Oh no! I'm going to get the axe!" she imagined. Her knees started shaking.

"…and we're very happy to present you with not only your Private Investigator's license, your very own set of handcuffs, but also your Concealed Carry permit." With that, Lou gave her a big smile as he handed over the items.

Sue was speechless as she stared at her license in a black leather bi-fold case and the cold, metal handcuffs in her hands. Kelsey and Monica started clapping and laughing then came over to her to hug her.

"Congratulations!" cheered Kelsey.

"Now you're one of us," said Monica with a wink of her eye.

At Monica's comment, Sue relaxed and started laughing, thinking about their pajama party.

"Oh my gosh! I wasn't expecting this! Thank you so much. Thank you, Lou!" she gushed.

"You're very welcome, Sue," Lou said. "Good job. Just keep up your workouts at the gym and target practice."

"Wow. It's just sinking in," Sue shook her head in disbelief then looked at her co-workers. "I'm a P.I.!" she announced.

"Hahaha!" they all laughed.

❧ 52 ❧

S ue, feeling confident and exuberant after getting her P.I. license and seeing her first case solved, drove to Maxim's apartment to celebrate. There, she planned to let herself in and make a romantic dinner for the two of them before he got home. In her mind's eye, they would stand close to each other, kissing, for an extended length of time until they eventually moved to his bed. She had never been in another man's bed before. It was thrilling to imagine and Sue looked forward to it. She could barely stand the wait.

She parked her SUV directly in front of the large apartment house in the middle of the Park Avenue area. It was *the* place to live with many restaurants, bars, shops, and art galleries within walking distance. It drew many intellectuals as well as first-time apartment dwellers. There was something for everyone there.

Grabbing a bag of groceries, she climbed the stairs to the second story and inserted the key Maxim had given her and opened the door.

The apartment was empty—totally empty—except for an envelope on the floor.

Fear had already erupted in her belly before she saw her name on the envelope. Where was Maxim?

Why didn't he tell her that he was moving? Or, was it something more final? Had he left her? Her hands trembled as she opened the envelope and the folded letter. It read:

"Dearest Sue,"

"I know you are shocked at this moment. I am sorry. I received a call from an agency in Washington, D.C., about a highly classified job. Since I have a government clearance, they requested me for an immediate assignment. I can't discuss it, but I had to leave quickly.

"Congratulations on your recent case. You are going to be a very successful detective and I am so very proud of you.

"You are asking yourself, 'What about us?' Well, if we are meant to be, we will be. I just can't be there now. I know we love each other, and we may still have a future, but I don't know how long I will need to stay in Washington. I can't expect you to wait for me or follow me since you just began your journey in Rochester.

"I know you need an apartment. I paid my rent for a year. Feel free to move in. I gave the landlord your phone number and she will call you in the next few days. Who knows? Maybe I'll be back soon.

"I will never forget you, Sue."

"Love, Maxim"

Sue fell to her knees clutching the note and sobbed, "No, no! This can't be! How could he do this to me?" When the tears finally stopped, she stuffed the note into her pocket.

She heard someone climbing the stairs! She called out with hope and anticipation, "Maxim?"

Instead of Maxim, it was Monica. "Sue!" she cried with a look of concern. "I saw your car parked outside. I just heard about Maxim myself. Oh, Sue! I'm so sorry!"

Sue got up off of her knees and went into Monica's arms, feeling the warmth and comfort of her generous breasts, where she wept again for several minutes. Just the sight of Maxim's sister made her feel the pain all over again. Monica stroked her hair and kissed her head and eyes. "I'm so sorry, Sue. Would you like to go out for a drink or have dinner with me and Kelsey? You could use some love."

She recalled the last time she spent time with Monica and Kelsey and she braved a bit of a smile. Then she just shook her head as she wiped away her tears with the back of her hand. "Thanks, but I have to go."

With that, Sue left Monica standing there and returned to her car to drive to the only place she could find solace—the cornfield where she and Maxim had made love recently.

The drive took about 20 minutes but, when she arrived, she was in for another shock. The corn had been harvested and, there, in the middle of the now-brown field were several construction vehicles and a large red-and-white sign announcing a new gas station and convenience store to be built soon. Sue went to the nearest parking lot and cried again. Memories were all she had left now. But they were happy times—no, joyous times—that she would never forget.

When Sue returned to her parents' house feeling abandoned and forlorn, there was a phone message for her. Officer Williams—Chris—called, asking if she would come to his backyard barbeque on July 4th. He was having family and friends over and he wanted to introduce her to everyone.

She wiped away a remaining tear, took a deep breath and let it out. Going to Chris' event would take her mind off Maxim, at least for a little while. Sue recalled Chris' intentions and she still felt uncomfortable about it. She considered Chris to be a work partner and not a love interest, but that could change if Maxim never came back. Sue returned the call from her bedroom.

"Hi, Chris. Sure, I'm free. Can I bring something?"

"Just bring yourself, Sue," Chris said. "I'd like you to meet my friends and colleagues."

"Okay. Sounds nice. See you then." She ended the call.

Turning to the teddy bear on her pillow, Sue thought, *"Maybe I can pick his mind about another unsolved murder."*

And so, another chapter in Sue's life began.

❦ 53 ❦

D an sat on his worn, swivel desk chair and turned on his computer. He carefully put in his password. Numerous files popped up. He put a thumb drive into the USB port and an icon appeared on his desktop. There were two folders inside that file. One was "Emily;" the other was "Dead Girl."

When he clicked on the Emily folder, there were numerous photos—some from her social media accounts that were intriguing and sexy. He touched the screen on her body.

But those weren't the images Dan liked best. When Emily came to his house and into his bedroom, there were cameras taking videos from different angles, of her turning the wooden box in various directions, trying to figure out the mysterious "trigger." Dan watched as he saw himself behind her, then, in one fast move, putting his hands under her top, feeling her breasts, kissing her neck, and the ensuing struggle over the bed. He winced when she kicked him, but it no longer hurt. He even found himself snickering.

Tonight, he watched the videos over and over, enjoying those exciting few minutes in total pleasure.

Then he switched to the other folder, the one he copied from the thumb drive inside the carved wooden box the first day he had it. The pictures weren't pretty, but to him they were titillating. And he smirked when he thought about that nosey female private detective warning him not to open the box. He felt he "had one over on her" and began to laugh—a sinister, loud, and hearty laugh.

"Hahahaha! Hahahaha! Hahahaha!"

He laughed so loudly that the sound carried outside and echoed against all the trees and buildings until it faded into the dark summer night like the ripples on the canal during that unholy night of murder.

About the Author

Elly Stevens was born and raised in Rochester, New York, in a family of storytellers. "Remember when..." were often the first words at every family gathering. At a very early age, Elly was writing fictional stories and scripts with characters from the 1950s TV shows like *The Thin Man* for her and her friends to act out.

Following her dream of writing, she joined the Publications group at Eastman Kodak Company where she held several positions including technical editor and the consumer-relationship management (CRM) team project manager for KODAK Digital Camera e-mail marketing campaigns. Elly retired in 2004.

It wasn't until a former co-worker, **Joe Janowicz,** contacted Elly to edit his first novel, ***Bang-Bang You're Dead,*** in 2018 that she picked up writing again.

Her first book, a memoir, ***Searching for Serenity in My Crazy Life,*** allows a peek into many of the real-life experiences with her family and friends. That book was followed by ***Dangerous Passion,*** a fictional story of fallible relationships, choices, passions, and ultimately... murder. ***Murder on the Erie Canal*** continues the story with detective-in-training and crime solver Sue Gainer, who finds herself in deep water with the killer.

https://www.AuthorEllyStevens.com

Ken Wheaton, Cover Artist

Murder on the Erie Canal cover designer **Ken Wheaton** also illustrated the cover of Elly Stevens' novel *Dangerous Passion*.

Ken also worked on comics for Bongo, IDW, Image, Moonstone, and Airwave. Most notably, he's contributed artwork to various *Simpsons* comics and books, as well as drawing several issues of *Popeye*. His other comic book work includes *Back to the Future, Official Adaptation of Mr. Magoo's Christmas Carol,* and issues of *I Dream of Jeannie, The Phantom, El Mucho Grande-Wrestler for Hire, Kolchak: The Night Stalker, Jetta,* and *Buckaroo Banzai—The Prequel.* He also drew a special commemorative premium comic celebrating the 80th birthday of cartoon icon *Popeye.* He was a contributing artist to the hardcover books *C. Montgomery Burns' Handbook of World Domination* and *Bart Simpson's Manual of Mischief.*

As a freelance illustrator, Ken contributed artwork and designs for a series of television ads for clients Toyota, McDonald's, and Wegmans.

He served as editor of *Munster Memories: A Coffin Table Book* with **Butch Patrick**. Ken illustrated two issues of the comic *Dreamer,* with creator **Joe Janowicz,** as well as editing and developing a revival anthology of the classic 1950's character *Jetta.*

Ken teaches several popular comic book production workshops each summer, which yield anthologies of student work and prepares tweens and teens interested in entering the field.

**More of Ken's work can be seen at
https://www.kenweaton.com**

DANGEROUS PASSION

By Elly Stevens

When obsession turns to murder!

It started with a seemingly innocent goodnight kiss... Innocent, until one person's desire ignited a firestorm of passions leading to a disastrous chain of events.

When a prostitute is murdered, the police think they have their man. But do they? Will the evidence reveal the real killer? Or will the killer remain at large? Love, lust, jealousy, hatred, revenge, and greed. All part of everyday life. And all motives for murder. You won't want to put down this fast-paced book until the very end.

**Available on Amazon and
Barnes and Noble online.
https://www.AuthorEllyStevens.com**

SEARCHING FOR SERENITY
in My Crazy Life

ELLY STEVENS

**The real-life stories of a baby boomer
in Rochester, New York.**

Everyone has a story to tell; **Elly Stevens** has a "lifetime" of stories to tell. Journey down memory lane as Elly recalls stories with her family and friends. Travel with her through every significant stage of her life and the beginning of new "life" at age 70.

Searching for Serenity in My Crazy Life. Fun, fascinating, and memory provoking. Growing up doesn't mean growing old. Growing up is a life story.

**Available on Amazon and
Barnes and Noble online.
https://www.AuthorEllyStevens.com**

THE NAKED DEAD

By Joe Janowicz

When the clothes come off, the killing begins.

Someone is killing naked people. Paradise Lost, an international naturist resort, is holding a major "bare all" nudist and adult swingers convention. When a celebrity guest is found floating "bottoms up" in one of the luxury outdoor pools, the local police are called to investigate. Another naked guest is found dead in the window display of an on-premise concessions shop. Both victims have bite marks in their necks and are drained of all their blood. Is this the work of a "real life" vampire, or a crazed psychopath pretending to be a vampire?

Detective Jamie Parker and Police Officer Jim McKenna are given the undercover assignment to stay on site as a couple and search for any clues. To blend in, they have to go "au natural" and mingle with the guests.

More mysterious deaths continue as the killer plays a game of cat and mouse with Jamie, intending to make her a victim. Never having been to a nudist resort, let alone walk around in public wearing only sunglasses and a smile, Jamie discovers that you don't need clothes to catch a killer.

Amazon online and selected bookstores
https://www.JoeJanowiczAuthor.com

Coming Soon!

GHOSTS
By Joe Janowicz

It is said that, amid the strange sounds of night, Ghosts roam the dark, seeking an escape, seeking peace, seeking their final destination. Death.

A haunted house, two mysterious authors, an open grave, a mysterious woman with no past, and someone, or something, is trying to find life after death.

GHOSTS

A new horror story from **Joe Janowicz,** author of **The Naked Dead**.

Even Ghosts Fall in Love.

For updates,
https://www.JoeJanowiczAuthor.com

www.ingramcontent.com/pod-product-compliance
Lightning Source LLC
Chambersburg PA
CBHW070518100726
47907CB00004B/890